Wicked Hill

a novella by

Ed Sams

MINT HILL BOOKS
MAIN STREET RAG PUBLISHING COMPANY
CHARLOTTE, NORTH CAROLINA

Special Thanks

My thanks to readers Rick Botelho and Ellen Young for their insightful critiques. Thanks goes to the Tennessee Writers Alliance for its encouragement in awarding me second place in its 2008 fiction contest for Nashville's Festival of Books. Thanks to San Jose State University for its Master of Fine Arts Program in Creative Writing. Thanks to the Yellow Tulip Press for the loan of its printer. Finally, my thanks to Sally Sams for her proofreading and Paul Douglass for his advice.

Library of Congress Control Number: 2012944322

ISBN: 978-1-59948-372-6

Produced in the United States of America

Mint Hill Books
Main Street Rag Publishing Company
PO Box 690100
Charlotte, NC 28227
www.MainStreetRag.com

For my sister, Sydney,
who showed me the way
to Wicked Hill

CONTENTS

CHAPTER I: UP WICKED HILL

If a black cat crosses one's path this is an omen of bad luck.

—Vergilius Ferm

The sun was setting as I began my climb up Wicked Hill. The farmer with the white horse who gave me a ride from the depot stopped at the foot bridge. "No men are allowed on Wicked Hill," he said. I looked down on the riling water racing beneath my feet. Allowed or not, I wondered how he could get his horse and wagon to ford that stream.

"What is the name of that river?" I asked him.

Ain't got a name, I'm told.

The farmer handed me my bag. "I come along this way every Saturday to market," he said. "Whenever you're ready to leave, come sun up of a Saturday, I'll be along."

I nodded, knowing that there would be no way I would leave Wicked Hill, for I had no money and nowhere to go. A hired girl must be particular of the company she keeps, so I just smiled at the farmer. I stroked the nose of his white horse for luck and waved as the wagon rolled on by. A hired girl must keep her counsel and keep her wages if she's to get on in the world.

That's what I was now. No longer Amy Scoggins, the pride of the church choir and darling of the congregation, just Amy Scoggins, some poor orphan girl from Fool's Gap.

In my bag was a crumpled letter from Miss Juanita Jenkins, the choir leader, speaking of my hard work, and another from Preacher Snodgrass speaking to my good character. I had no way of knowing if the job had been filled or even if I was what she was looking for, but I was ready to please Miss Wicks as soon as I laid eyes on her. I was a pleaser. I would make her pleased with me just as I had everyone in Fool's Gap.

The way up Wicked Hill was rocky and steep. The road was no more than wheel ruts, and on either side the pastures were knee deep in weeds. Nothing but weeds and the little wandering breeze passing through the brush with blue blossoms that clung to the hillside.

It was dusk when I reached the farmhouse on Wicked Hill. There before me was a big double-story house of brick with three pillars in front holding up to another little porch on top. I lifted my eyes in the half light for a row of little windows on the pitch of the roof which must be the attic. One of those little windows might look out a room that was going to be mine. Just a bed and a table and a chair—and dust—but enough, God willing, for Amy Scoggins.

Squaring my shoulders I marched up to the wide front door and rapped the heavy bronze knocker. I waited, as you do, not to be bold, just ready to let whoever's inside know you're there. After counting to ten, I rapped once more, this time a little longer and a little harder. I put my little ear up to the door. No sound at all. Not even an echo. Stepping back into the dooryard I noticed no light coming from any of the windows. Is anyone to home?

Then I heard the sounds of groaning as the big front door scraped open and a black cat jumped out of the darkness. I ran off the steps as the cat hissed and arched its back at my feet.

"Who's there?" came a gruff voice from the doorway.

"It's me, Ma'am. Amy Scoggins. Miss Juanita Jenkins sent me. I'm your new hired girl."

"I'll decide that," came the voice in the darkness. "Tabitha, shoo!"

The black cat ran off in the night and I hurried inside. All was gloom in the long hall I stepped into. There was no telling where I was or who was there in the dark.

"Well," said the voice crossly, "if you are hired to help, help me get some light in here. I was commencing to light the lamps when I was interrupted by the knock at the door."

Now I felt foolish to be the cause of the darkness that so afeared me, but no doubt that was the old voice's purpose. To put me in my place. I simpered a little to let her know I was smiling there in the dark and said sweet as pie, "Yes, Ma'am. I'm here to help, and I am very good at trimming lamps. No smoke, no lampblack with the way I get them lit. Just show the way, please, and there will be light here soon enough."

"Gabby little thing," the old voice commented by reply.

I walked on in the darkness following what seemed to be a big black lump of meanness down that long dark hallway which finally turned into a pantry with a banked hearth.

I followed that mean old voice into the light of the dying fire. It belonged to a large shapeless old woman who heaved herself down in a rocking chair. The chair groaned with her weight.

"Now if I only had a reaching stick," the old woman sighed.

"I'm here to help. Ma'am," I said all perky.

"Then fetch me my snuffbox there on the cupboard."

I made my way through the dusty darkness looking for something like a cupboard that might hold a snuffbox. I went past the pie safe next to the dry sink and followed the pie rail over to what seemed to be the cupboard. Feeling around, I found a little hinged box that I took to her. She accepted it with a grunt.

Looking around for any food left out, I commented, "If there are any leftovers from dinner that I could put away...."

"I thought you were going to trim the lights," she interrupted.

"Yes, Ma'am," I said and got started. I pulled down the ceiling lamp. There was still oil in it. I snatched a broom straw from an old besom next to the hearth and caught it afire, and lifting the hurricane glass I lit the kerosene wick. That whole dark room filled with light. I turned to my mistress and smiled.

My! What an ugly old woman she was. One long woolly brow across both piggy eyes. Warts around her neck. Swollen hands and feet. Bands of fat spread out in puddles spilling from her body. She did not smile back.

"There's a candle over there you could light," she said.

I took the broom straw and lit it in the kerosene wick and carried it to the candle on the shelf at the hallway. No sign of food anywhere.

Turning to my new mistress, I smiled once again. "I haven't eaten since this morning and I was hoping before it got too late...."

"Yes?" Her voice sounded guarded.

"That I might have my supper, Ma'am."

"You had best take that up with your mistress, girl."

"But aren't you? I mean, aren't you Miss Wicks?"

"That I am," the old girl nodded, digging into her snuffbox. "But I sent out no inquiries for hired girls. You must want my sister, Miss Marietta. I am Miss Henrietta Wicks."

"But why?" I started to complain, then saw the first sign of a smile sprout from her cracked lips. She was all eyes and ears ready to hear me out. I stopped and started again, "But where is she, Ma'am? I should see her before it gets too late."

"That you should," the old girl nodded. She took her time poking the black snuff into her lower gums. Then she spoke up once again. "Take the backdoor and follow the path by the henhouse before it gets too dark. The path will take you through the woods to the cabin in the clearing."

I looked out the window at the dark. "Perhaps, I could borrow a lantern to show me the way," I asked.

She raised her long woolly brow in surprise. "I don't lend my property to others," she said, "no matter how they simper and smile."

With that I gathered my bag and was off into the dark. The moon was beginning to peek over the mountaintop. There was enough light for me to find the henhouse where the soft clucking sounds of sleeping chickens I found strangely soothing. From there I saw the path that led down through the tall trees that swayed in the wind above. Under my feet I could hear the earth itself moaning as the wind shivered through me. Before long I came to the clearing.

There stood a pretty little cabin with a light shining in the window and trail of smoke coming from the chimney. On the wide porch were dried gourds and flowers hanging from its rafters. I marched up to knock on the door. Then out of the darkness, across my path, there snarled that same black cat that beset me at the farmhouse. I let out a yell and critter bounded off into the dark.

The door of the cabin opened a crack. "Who's there?" A sharp, shrill voice commanded.

"If you please, Ma'am, are you Miss Marietta Wicks?" I called nearly pleading.

"Who asks?" came the guarded reply.

"Amy Scoggins," I said. "I'm your new hired girl you sent for." I started digging in my bag for the letters that would square the matter.

"Come to light, so I might see you," the bird-like voice told me.

Gathering my bag and letters I walked up to the door, which the person inside opened wide enough for me to enter. The room was white-washed with rose chintz curtains and little china dishes all around. A goodly fire danced in the fireplace. I spied another room behind the hearth. All in all, a cozier trade than that farmhouse.

"I've been expecting you."

I turned and faced the silver-haired little lady as thin as a broom straw, just as skinny and slight as her sister was big and fat.

"Let me look at you, girl," she said, her face wrinkled with smiles. I smiled back. "My, you are a pretty thing!" she cooed. "So young! Is this your first time for hire?"

"Oh, no, Ma'am. I was a year hired out to Miss Juanita Jenkins who penned this here letter listing all I done for her." I grabbed the letter from my bag and pushed it in her hand.

The little lady did no more than glance at it. She seemed content to stare at me instead. "And what are your skills, my dear?" she asked.

I gulped and launched into a long budget of chores that Miss Juanita had me do. "I can cook," I began.

"We have a cook," she said.

I gulped again. "I sweep, scrub, mop, sew a little, wash windows, and the baseboards, clean fireplaces and haul ashes, do the laundry and the ironing, bleaching and bluing, rake leaves, shovel snow, pull weeds, and help with the canning," I said, drawing breath.

"Goodness!" the sweet voice sighed. "If you did so much for this Miss Jenkins, I am surprised she could part with you."

"She didn't, Ma'am. I stayed with her until the end and then I stayed to bury her."

Those pale, cloudy blue eyes widened. "You buried her yourself?"

"I laid her out as I did my own maw and paw the winter before."

"To lose both parents in one year, my, my, my!"

"Yes'm," I said, "First Paw took to the fever, then Maw got the palsy and died shortly after."

My new mistress shook her head sadly. "An orphan all alone in the world!" she marveled. Then she smiled. "You're just what I was looking for."

I heaved a sigh of relief. "I am glad to serve you, Ma'am. I hope I can earn my ten dollars by year's end."

"To be sure, my dear."

"Of course, that's on top of my bed and board." I paused, then asked. "I will board here, won't I?"

"To be sure, to be sure."

I heaved a little sigh, looking around for signs of a meal.

"I shall take my meals with you, Ma'm?" I asked.

"If you wish to bear me company, my love."

"I'd bear you company right now, if there was anything to eat," I said.

That sweet old lady sighed once again. "I'm afraid the evening dishes have been put away." She smiled at me fondly.

"Oh," I said, not bothering to hide my disappointment. Then I began again. "And my bed, Ma'am. Where would you have me sleep?"

Suddenly that friendly face wrinkled up and turned pale. "You surely can't expect to sleep here!" she cried. "I can't abide the thought of anyone watching me while I sleep."

"Well, where then?" I asked. "Your sister's house?"

"Oh, I don't think she would like that either."

"Then where? The hen house!"

"Certainly not!" Miss Marietta snapped. "And I don't care for your tone. The help sleep in the cookhouse. You must go there."

"And where is that, please?" I asked, tired and hungry but still smiling.

"Follow the footpath back to farmhouse then take the fork to the right. It's by the barn near the cowshed."

"Yes, Ma'm," I said picking up my carpetbag once more.

Miss Marietta hurried to the door. "I would rush if I were you. It's getting late. We go to bed with the chickens here on Wicked Hill. You would not want to wake the cook and have her cross." With that last word of advice, she closed the door behind her and I was left in the dark once again.

The moon was high overhead as I made my way back up the footpath and past the dreaming chickens in the warm straw of the henhouse. I followed the fork to the right which wound around a large barn where the wind was whipping through the trees and the ground underneath was groaning with every weary step I took.

There was the cookhouse. No smoke in the chimney but a light still on. I hurried up to the step and rapped on the double Dutch door.

"Yes?" The top half of the Dutch door swung open and a face like an ax blade thrust itself out into the night.

"If you please, Ma'am, I'm the new hired girl. I was sent her to find my bed and supper."

"You're in luck. Dinner is put away and the dishes washed, but there is bread and butter. I'll get you a glass of milk."

"Thank you, Ma'am," I said and fell into her arms.

The cook, Mistress Fortune, led me inside and took my bag. "Sit by the fire. I'll be no more than a minute with a plate for you." She was as good as her word. Soon there by the fire, I ate from a Blue Willow plate with a foamy glass of milk by my side.

Mistress Fortune sat on the stool across from me. "Now tell me all about yourself," she said. So I told her the same sad story that got me nowhere with the two old sisters before.

"Pay them no mind, Amy Scoggins. They can think of no one but themselves. You must get used to their ways if you plan to stay here."

"Stay I must. I have nowheres to go."

Mistress Fortune frowned. "You'll leave," she said. "They all leave, one way or another. Don't think you're the first. You'll be gone by the spring thaws."

"I'll not leave without my pay," I said. "I've been promised ten dollars at year's end along with bed and board."

"You'll earn it!" Mistress Fortune replied. "Remember you work for Miss Marietta, but Miss Henrietta will have you do for her too, if I know her."

"She already has!" I said remembering the lamps and the snuffbox.

"She should pay as well then. Not much, of course, since you share her bed and board."

"Coppers are always welcome," I said coyly.

"Aye," said Mistress Fortune, "so they are. Then take your ten dollars at year's end, if you last that long, and all the coppers you get in between. But listen to me, Amy Scoggins, whatever is said, take not the silver penny."

"But a silver penny is worth ten coppers," I argued.

"Listen to me, Amy Scoggins, take not the silver penny however much they wheedle and cry."

"The two sisters will want me to take a silver penny?"

Mistress Fortune nodded sternly. "That's why you must not!"

As she spoke, the ground itself underneath our feet began to shudder and all around outside there came a low, mournful moan.

I jumped up from the chair where I sat. "What's that!" I cried.

Mistress Fortune smiled for the first time that night. "You'll get used to it. It has a life of its own and a sad one."

"What does?" I asked.

Mistress Fortune looked out the window into the dark. "Wicked Hill."

CHAPTER II: WICKED GAMES

If you are about to break a witch's charm, she can break your charm, provided she or a member of her family borrows anything from you or your family.

—2001 Southern Superstitions

Mistress Fortune tucked me in snug and dry in the loft behind the hearth of the cookhouse and there I slept dreamlessly, but woke at first light before cockcrow. The moaning and sighing of Wicked Hill stirred me from my slumbers.

"Why does the land around here make such racket?" I asked the cook as I came down the steps to the kitchen.

Mistress Fortune looked up from the pot she had on the boil. "It's not the land so much as the waters that rush by it, ever eating away at all they touch."

I remembered the riling water under the foot bridge on my way up Wicked Hill. "What's the name of the river that runs by here?" I asked.

"Not got a name," said Mistress Fortune. "Folks tend to ignore it and stay clear. Every spring it rushes over its banks and bears all away that it can. It's an all-devouring river that's got no name, and it will one day bear away Wicked Hill, you mark my words."

With that, Mistress Fortune handed me a pail and sent me to the cowshed. It was still dark out so I took the pour lamp made from an old tin pitcher. The pitcher had little holes punched in its sides all round for the light to pour out from the lamp. Up the hill in the cowshed I found the sweetest brown Guernsey cow I had ever set eyes on. I spent more time than I ought stroking that soft smooth nose and gazing into those sweet brown eyes. An old rooster woke me out of my daze and I hurried back to the cookhouse with the fresh milk.

"Wash your face and hands," said the cook, "and take an apron from the press. I got Miss Marietta's breakfast ready. It's here on the covered tray. Take the path back up to the henhouse and then back down to the cabin. Don't cut across the birch field. Poison ivy grows there."

I skipped along with the tray that hardly felt any weight at all. I wondered what Miss Marietta must eat that feels so slight. No wonder she was no more than skin and bones. When I got to the cabin, I rapped on the door and was told to come in, for the door was on the latch. Inside my lady was still abed, but looking pretty as a picture with her silver curls popping out of her gingham night cap.

"Oh, Goody!" she cried and clapped her hands as she lifted the covered dish on the tray. "More mush for me." She nibbled daintily on her tiny silver spoon. "Not even a dash of salt for seasoning. Old Peachie never disappoints." She thrust the tray aside.

"Old Peachie, Ma'am?" I asked learning all I could.

My lady noticed me for the first time today. "I hope you are settling in, my child. Old Peachie taking good care of you?" She saw my blank stare and seemed satisfied. "What is your name again?"

"Amy. Amy Scoggins, Ma'am. Actually my christened name is Annamay but my friends all call me Amy."

"Well, girl," said Miss Marietta, giving up on remembering so much, "have you been to the henhouse yet?"

"I'm to fetch you ladies breakfast before I start my dirty chores."

"Then I should like very much if you would bring me a pocket full of feathers from my sister's fine Holland layers.

I plan to stay indoors today and finish my fire screen." She waved a scrawny wrist in the direction of the mantel where a fancy frame of broidery stood. "No need to mention this to my sister. She is so jealous of her fine Holland layers that she might begrudge you a few feathers."

"Least said soonest mended," I said and she smiled.

I hurried back to the cookhouse going up the path by the henhouse and then down the path by the barn carrying the covered dish on the covered tray. Once I got back to the kitchen, Mistress Fortune had Miss Henrietta's meal ready for me to take.

"Better go to the press and grab a mob to hide those curls. You wouldn't want Miss Henrietta Wicks to find hair in her food."

I glanced at my face in the window and shook my head to see my curls dance. I sighed. It was the Sabbath. The thought of church back in Fool's Gap came on me all of a sudden and saddened me. I sighed once more.

"What ails you, Amy Scoggins?" Mistress Fortune asked me.

I turned from the window. "Is there no church-going here on Wicked Hill?"

"None at all, Amy Scoggins, and the less said about that the better you will get along here."

I nodded and tried to smile. "It's just that every Sunday in Fool's Gap I would scrub my face to make it shine and shake my curls out and wear this little Polly gown I got for Sunday go a meeting. Even Preacher Snodgrass would say how Christian I looked."

"There's no pew sitting nor Bible thumping here on Wicked Hill," said Mistress Fortune sternly. "The two misses wouldn't stand for it. Now hurry this tray to Miss Henrietta afore the food gets cold."

I took the tray, but could not hurry, for this tray was as heavy as the other had been light, heavy with dishes of eggs and sausages, fried apples and cathead biscuits along with a china boat of red-eyed gravy.

In the farmhouse I found my lady not in the dining room or the front parlor or even in the best bedroom down the hall. "In here," came a mean old voice down the dim hallway. There was a little room in the back filled with books and in an overstuffed chair in the corner sat Miss Henrietta, looking as though there she had slept through the night. I set the tray on a side table next to the chair and removed the cloth. That old black cat sat in her lap staring up at me.

"Tabitha, shoo!" said my lady, spilling the cat to the floor.

Two yellow eyes looked up at me and glared as though blaming me for the injury. With a hiss and a spit, Tabitha leapt from the room. I looked up at Miss Henrietta. Not another word did she say, nor one look she gave me, but instantly set upon the food taking it all with both hands. I let myself out.

In the henhouse I found an egg basket where Mistress Fortune told me to look and I commenced a gathering eggs. My poor paw tried raising leghorns but the raccoons ate them, and Miss Henrietta Jenkins had a fine flock of Rhode Island Reds until she died, but neither were as handsome as Miss Henrietta Wick's Holland Blue. The eggs were large and white and still warm to the touch. Deep blue feathers stuck out from the straw. As I left the henhouse with a basket full of eggs and a fist full of feathers, something glinting in the morning sunlight caught my eye. There on the path behind the farmhouse was what appeared to be a pin!

"See a pin and pick it up," Miss Juanita Jenkins would say, "and all the day you'll have good luck."

I set the egg basket down in the soft sand and fished up the steel pin which I cleaned with my apron and pushed through the apron strap just above my heart. I reached down for the egg basket when I noticed Miss Wicks staring at me from the back porch.

"Come here, girl," she said. "When next you go to the cabin, look sharp for an old leather book with speckles on the cover. It's a book of recipes my sister borrowed and I want it back. No need to tell my sister. She gets so particular about trifles."

When I did not move, she added, "There may be a silver penny for you if you fetch it afore dinner."

I returned to the cookhouse with the basket of eggs and Mistress Fortune set me to churning butter, only the butter would not churn, so she sent me to fetch the chamber pots, and then the dishes, and then the laundry of both ladies. Miss Marietta, for such a dainty thing, used a passel of dish cloths and wash cloths and fine hosiery. I was struggling with a big wash basket when she called me to her side.

"Did you remember the feathers?" she asked.

"I clean forgot I had them," I said, reaching into my apron pocket for the deep blue feathers.

"Clever girl!" she cried, taking them in both hands.

"I could have picked some off the ground, but I figgered for the fire screen you would want them fresh, so I plucked from the empty nests."

"Where did you come by that, my love?"

I saw Miss Marietta's eyes glittering as she stared hard just above my heart, which stopped for a split second, so sharp was the look she gave me.

"It's a pin I found out back of the farmhouse," I told her.

"May I borrow it for awhile?" Miss Marietta simpered. "I'll need it to hold the feathers to the fire screen as I sew them on."

"I guess we're friends enough to borrow," I said handing her the pin.

Miss Marietta nodded. "Oh, yes, we are always borrowing from one another here on Wicked Hill."

Then I left not feeling bad at all in taking the book with the speckled cover I found in the drawer where I put her hose. Miss Henrietta was ever so glad to get her book. She reached into her reticule and pulled out a silver penny.

I shook my head. "I'll take a copper instead."

"Foolish girl, do you not know a silver penny is worth ten coppers?"

"Yes, ma'am, but I'll not take a silver penny, only a copper or none at all."

Begrudgingly she thrust the copper in my palm, but her generosity did her no good. Starting that day her prize Hollands stopped laying.

CHAPTER III: THE WITCH EGG

"A witch can obtain butter by merely squeezing the handle of an ordinary table fork."

—2001 *Southern Superstitions*

Perhaps there's a weasel."

I had come from the henhouse that next morning with no eggs in my basket.

"Were there signs of a weasel?" Mistress Fortune asked.

I thought a bit and shook my head. "No chicks kilt, no eggs sucked dry."

"And no eggs at all?" Mistress Fortune asked.

"Well, I left one egg under each hen to keep her laying," I said.

"Good girl! An odd number is lucky for egg laying."

"But if there is a weasel," I asked, "what's to be done to catch it?"

"Why, what would you do with a weasel if you caught it? Think, girl! And while you're at it, fetch one of the eggs from the larder."

I did as I was told, and Mistress Fortune took it over to the hearth. Bending low in the ashes from the morning fire, she marked a cross on the egg with soot.

"There," she said, handing me the old sooty egg, "put this marked egg by the door to the henhouse and no weasel will bother the chickens again."

But the next day the single eggs left in the nests had disappeared as well. Mistress Fortune made a special trip to the henhouse to see to the matter herself and came away confused.

"I've not seen the like of it," she confided. "Get me the stone jug from the pantry and we'll put corn mash in their feed. That should perk them up!"

For two days I watched drunken Blue Hollands weaving through the barnyard flapping their wings in vain and never getting off the ground. Their nests lay bare and cold.

Meanwhile there were plenty of eggs and still much butter in the larder, so Mistress Fortune continued with her fine meals for one sister and her spare meals for the other. For Miss Henrietta there was flummeries and fools, puddings, and syllabubs and nogs, and for Miss Marietta molasses and mush.

Once I asked the cook why the sisters were fed such different meals. "It's all a matter of knowing what's good for you, Amy Scoggins," Mistress Fortune said. "It's safest to keep Miss Marietta on thin gruel and weak tea, while it's best to keep Miss Henrietta well fed." But that was still early in the week.

After three days we were beginning to run low on fresh eggs, and Miss Henrietta had to be told. Mistress Fortune and I went together. We waited on her in the little back room filled with books. There she poured over blueprints on pendulums and hated to be interrupted.

"Sing to them!" she cried and turned back to her ciphering.

"You're a chorister," Mistress Fortune told me. "You sing to them, just no hymns."

Which was fine by me, for I knew plenty of songs, jolly ones like "The Bride Who Couldn't Make Cornbread" or sad ones like "Wedding Day Shoot Out." I could sing a blue streak, and honestly did not mind singing all day so long as it got me out of my other chores, but only a full morning of my singing was all that Miss Henrietta could take.

"Come here, girl," she said to me just as I started up another ballad. I came to where she sat cleaning a shotgun on the back porch of the farmhouse. "Don't you know singing is bad for the heart?" she asked me.

I shook my head no.

"It might be, if you sing one more song, and this gun goes off and shoots you there!"

We both decided then and there that I had sung enough for one day, and yet that singing was not enough, for still the Blue Hollands would not lay.

As the days passed, I noticed strange changes in the two sisters. Miss Henrietta, usually so fat and high colored, began to look thin in the face and peaked, while Miss Marietta, no bigger than a minute, began to plump up. She started to take walks, twirling a yellow silk parasol past the henhouse singing "Ta Ra Ra Boom De Yay" until Miss Henrietta yelled out the back window for her to stop.

We were so worried about the hens not laying that it wasn't until the end of the week that we realized that butter refused to churn. Mistress Fortune was determined not to let her kitchen be without eggs and butter. "We can do nothing about the hens, drat them! But we can stay here and churn until Doomsday if need be!"

So we spelled each other. As one's arms got tired, the other would take over. "Sing your hymns, Amy Scoggins," Mistress Fortune said in desperation.

So I sang every hymn I knew and then I sang some that I made up on the spot. When I got to the old "One Hundred and One," Mistress Fortune stopped me. "Better go to the barn and look for the old horse bridle. No doubt it's in the tack room next to the workshop."

The barn was bigger than the farmhouse it stood behind. It had windows all about and a little glass tower on top with a crooked weathervane. There were no horses on Wicked Hill, but the barn at one point had clearly been a stable. Only now the long dogtrot from the front to the back had been turned into a workshop. And such a workshop as I had never seen! Big slabs of limestone impossible to move were left lying about. Some had writing on them. Others seemed to have faces. Tools were spread all about—hammers and mallets, drills, braces, and drill bits. I nearly forgot the bridle looking at the nuts, and bolts, and screws, not just flatheads and cross-cuts, but some like sunbursts and starlights.

"What work is done in the workshop?" I asked Mistress Fortune when I returned with the bridle.

"Oh, none now that all the men have been run off Wicked Hill," Mistress Fortune replied. "We had one here who was as clever a stone cutter as ever I saw. He was a locksmith too. Those tools were his. The two sisters ran him off the day after my old Mam was buried. They could not abide him here any longer."

"Who was your old mam?" I asked.

Mistress Fortune stopped her work at the churn to wipe a hair from her hatchet face. "The same old mam as was Miss Henrietta's and Miss Marietta's. I was a foundling left in a peach basket at the footbridge of Wicked Hill," she said, looking far off, as though in the distance she could see it all happening again. "My old Mam raised me as one of her own. Twas she who named me Peachie Fortune, for I was fortune's child and Peachie. . . ."

"Because of the basket?" I asked.

"Because I was as pretty as a peach, she said," Mistress Fortune told me. "I always had better color than Miss Marietta, who was sallow, or Miss Henrietta, who was choleric. We three studied together at our mother's knee and I was always the quick one with my lessons. 'Listen, Peachie,' my old Mam would tell me, 'Life is not fair, but you are not of my blood, though you are child of my heart. Once I am gone, you must stay to look after those two sad cases that sprung from my loins, for I fear what my own daughters might do to each other once I am gone.' And no sooner had she died than all the men were run off Wicked Hill, but I stayed behind true to my old Mam and her word."

Peachie Fortune took the bridle and placed it over the butter churn. "Try now, Amy Scoggins. See if the butter don't come."

To my surprise, so it did.

I learned many things from Peachie Fortune. Plant nasturtiums on St. Patrick's Day. Plant beans on Good Friday. Never plant anything on the first three days of May, for these are barren days. Plant cucumbers on the Fourth of July.

But still the hens wouldn't lay, and now the Guernsey I called Brownie Belle went dry. Everything seemed to go awry. The hand pump in the cookhouse needed to be primed. There between the barn and the cowshed was the well with a well sweep and bucket for drawing water. We had to draw water from the well to prime the pump and then use that water for recipes that called for milk. The cook and I would go together to bring in enough water for the day's work.

"Were you the first of the hired girls here on Wicked Hill?" I asked.

Peachie Fortune turned the well sweep. "I never thought of it that way, but of course you are right. I have been nothing but the hired girl all these years to any of them."

"Have there been many hired girls?" I asked.

"Lands, yes! We have gone through the flower names, Rose, and Violet, and Lily; then the jewel names, Ruby, and Pearl, and Opal; and then came the virtues, Grace, and Patience, and Prudence. None stayed past the spring thaw. Not even the last one, Doris Sawyer, who never said good-bye. None had the grit."

I would stay past the spring thaw, though I did not say so. I knew I would stay, not because I had the grit, but just because I had no other place to go. Here was to be my home on Wicked Hill where butter was hard to come by and there were no eggs.

Until one day about week after the hens stopped laying, I peeped inside the henhouse just to see. There in the bright glare of midmorning I spied in the farthest nest a queer little egg with a gray cast to the shell. But it was an egg nonetheless!

I ran off to tell Peachie Fortune the news. There sauntering past the barnyard was Miss Marietta decked in all her finery twirling her yellow parasol and singing in a high shrill voice, "Polly Wolly Doodle." Somehow she had only grown stronger this past week of privation.

When Peachie Fortune took the egg from me, she frowned. "This is no good," she said. "We must go tell Miss Henrietta what you found." Up we trooped past the barn and barnyard and Miss Marietta singing to the chickens and entered the backdoor of the farmhouse that was left ajar.

We found Miss Henrietta in the backroom full of books sitting in that overstuffed chair with the black cat on her lap.

"Tabitha, shoo!" she cried and stood up to examine the egg. "Bring me that candy dish on the side table." I got the dish and held it as she cracked the wee, queer egg to pour the innards out. It was yolkless!

I gasped. "A witch egg!" The words tumbled out without my meaning to speak. Both my lady and her cook turned to me and frowned.

"We do not use that word here on Wicked Hill," Miss Henrietta told me.

Peachie Fortune cleared her throat. "We had to put the bridle over the butter churn."

My lady's mouth dropped open, and I noticed once more how the folds of fat hung sadly down her neck and her eyes were all hollow. "This is bad, Mistress Fortune, but I don't see how...." She stopped midsentence and cocked her ear to the window. Outside we heard Miss Marietta parading with her parasol singing "Nellie Bly."

"My sister is in a merry mood these days. I wonder what she's been up to." The lady and her cook turned to me and stared. I lowered my head, but I could feel the two sets of eyes bearing down on me.

"She's been working on her fire screen," I offered.

"Is that all?" asked Peachie Fortune.

"Yes'm," I assured them, "she must be getting ready to use the Holland feathers by now."

"My Holland feathers!" Miss Henrietta brayed.

"Well, the ones I found on the henhouse floor," I fibbed crossing my fingers.

Miss Henrietta eased herself back down in her chair. "But I still don't see how this could be since I have the book."

"No, ma'am," I said, trembling now, "I've seen her with the book," hoping neither knew how I fetched it for her.

"When was this, child?" Peachie Fortune asked.

I thought hard with both of them glaring at me. "The day after I fetched the feathers, Monday, I think."

Peachie Fortune frowned. "The day the cow went dry?"

Miss Henrietta's mouth dropped. "She's got the eggs and the butter!"

"We must consult the book," Peachie Fortune. She turned to me, "You now go quick and borrow it back."

I rushed out the room with Miss Henrietta saying, "Don't let her see you. Take the front door and circle around the hill," and Peachie Fortune calling, "But not the short cut through the birch field. There's poison ivy!"

Out the front door was the road I came up that first night on Wicked Hill. It wound past the farmhouse around the woods that circled the cabin before it came to an end on the windy side of Wicked Hill. Here was a cow path that led back down to the cabin. I got there in two shakes. Miss Marietta could still be heard singing in the distance.

The cabin had only a front room and a back room, but they were large and crowded with belongings. Rockers and dressers and chests and trays filled with broken locks and keys. The book with the speckled leather binding was not left out, so I had to snoop in boxes and peek in baskets and delve into drawers.

Snap! I clamped my right hand over my mouth to keep from crying and pulled out my left hand caught in a mouse trap. I pried it loose off my reddening hand and wondered just why it was there. I pulled out the drawer all the way, and there was the book with leather binding, the book of recipes.

Holding my sore hand in my mouth, I hurried back up the cow path and down the road and entered the farmhouse through the front way. Miss Henrietta snatched the book from my hands. Neither my lady nor her cook seemed to notice me at all as they pored over the pages of that hidebound book. Finally Miss Henrietta laid the book face down on the arm of her over-stuffed chair and hoisted herself to her feet.

"I need me a reaching stick," she said.

"You've got the book back," Peachie Fortune told her. "Wait and see."

"Help me to the window, Mistress Fortune, I have news for my sister."

As my lady and her cook made their way to the window, I set the book on the armchair to rights, but not before peeking inside. I don't know all my letters as I ought and I had but twinkling to see, but what I saw read something like this— *To break a witch's charm,* something something, *she can stop you* something something, *if she or her* something something *borrows anything from you or your* something something.

I could have found out more, but Peachie Fortune quietly drew the book from my hand and closed its speckled cover and laid it down on the arm of the chair.

Miss Henrietta turned from the window with a smug look. "That put a bug in her ear. Girl!" she said to me, "Go tend to your mistress. She'll want company I reckon and we want to know what she has to say."

Yet when I got to the cabin, Miss Marietta was humming sweetly to herself working on the fire screen. "Oh, there you are," she said when she saw me, "where's my book?"

"Your sister wished to borrow it once more and bid me fetch it," I said all fluttery.

Miss Marietta did not quite frown, nor quite smile either, but her mouth drew up not quite deciding which to do, so she spoke instead. "I suppose you are here to do as you are told," she sighed. "We can always borrow it back, I reckon, when she's not looking."

No more was said, so I went on with my chores around the cabin inside and out, and about sundown I set off up the winding path to bring Miss Marietta her supper. Suppers had turned sad on Wicked Hill now that there were no eggs nor butter. Peachie Fortune could still bake bread and fry potatoes with lard, so none would starve, but how we missed butter so! Except Miss Marietta who never complained about her meal and always cleaned her plate. I stood by the darkened window as night crept in, waiting for my lady to finish supper, and as I waited I sucked my sore fingers and watched.

For the first time I noticed how Miss Marietta ate. She chuckled to herself with every mouthful, stroking her empty knife against the slice of bread. I watched and moved closer to the light of the fire in the hearth to get a better look. I was not sure what I saw. I watched as Miss Marietta squeezed her knife and then stroked the bread, with butter pouring off the knife every time she squeezed it. Yellow butter ran down the knife and over the bread onto the Blue Willow plate, and then she would sop the butter up with the bread, wiping the plate clean before squeezing the knife to butter her potatoes.

As I watched this marvel before my eyes, I felt a shiver down my back like you get when someone is looking over your shoulder. I turned to the window, and there through the glass I saw the mean stare of the black cat Tabitha, those yellow eyes glowering, seeing all that I saw before bounding off into the night.

CHAPTER IV: THE REACHING STICK

The wand is a power, it controls Nature and bends the will of men.

—Vergilius Ferm

"Well?"

I shook my head.

Peachie Fortune snatched the milk pail and looked inside as if she doubted me.

"We must go to her," she said.

Off we marched up the path to the farmhouse with more bad news and entered by the backdoor. In the little back room filled with books stood Miss Henrietta, and in her armchair lay Tabitha, her black cat, as if she had slept there all night. Tabitha's yellow eyes looked up at us smugly.

Mistress Fortune and I stood at attention as Miss Henrietta fumed and fussed. She was in a mad mood already, without even hearing about her cow gone dry.

"Butter from her knife! She's stolen the butter and got the hens not to lay," thundered Miss Henrietta.

Peachie Fortune turned to me and frowned. I shrugged my shoulders. Who could I have told? No one but Peachie, yet somehow Miss Henrietta was on to Miss Marietta's trick.

"I have been pacing the night in perplexity," she roared. "What good is the book if it don't protect me!" She picked up the leatherbound book of recipes and threw it against the wall of books behind me. I ducked.

Peachie Fortune quickly got the book from where it fell, then turned to sooth her lady. Miss Henrietta waved her away.

"I don't understand. I sent that one," Miss Henrietta said pointing at me, "to borrow from my sister. That should have been enough protection."

"Unless, she or her helper borrowed from you," I said, finally seeing what the book meant.

Miss Henrietta turned toward me like a flash. Her eyes glared at me as if seeing something for the first time. Her gaze was just above my heart, which thumped in my chest.

"There's something different about you," said she, squinting. "There," she pointed. "Weren't there a pin you put on your apron strap, one you found in my barnyard?"

I began to shake. "Yes'm," I cried, whimpering a little.

"Where is it?" my lady demanded. Her keen dark eyes beneath the long woolly brow bore two holes in me.

I began to blubber. "I lent it to Miss Marietta cause she asked me to."

"A double jinx," Peachie Fortune said. "She's borrowed back from you. You've nothing on her."

Miss Henrietta flung out her arms with a shout and knocked me to the floor. I started to cry. Peachie Fortune helped me to my feet and told me to hush. She turned to face my lady.

"Control yourself. 'Tis but a pin! And you have the book. You'll have to read it now, but which would you rather have—a pin or the book?"

Miss Henrietta took the book her cook offered and pried it open and peered inside. "Hand me my change purse," she said.

Peachie Fortune went to the desk and opened the drawer and pulled forth a leather change purse with a metal clasp. Miss Henrietta pulled out a silver coin. We both stepped back.

My lady shook her head impatiently. "It's a silver dollar, a dollar," she cried waving the coin in front of us. "Take this to the whetstone in the workshop and sharpen its edge."

"What for?" I asked.

"To cut the tongue of the cow. Then she'll give milk."

"Not Brownie Belle!" I wailed.

That stopped Miss Henrietta in her tracks.

"It's the name the child gave the Guernsey," Peachie Fortune said.

"You're as bad as the last one," my lady told me. "What was her name? Doris Sawyer."

Peachie nodded, remembering, "Then the cow was called Brown Bess."

Miss Henrietta turned red in a passion. "That cow has got a name already, a first name and a last. The last name is COW and the first name is MINE!"

Peachie Fortune sighed. "You all will be the death of me someday, but I think I know a way to get the milk without hurting the cow. If we look, surely there'll be some sign to show that cow's been tampered with."

Miss Henrietta seemed to read her mind. "The Tether! Find it, Mistress Fortune. Release the tether and you will release the milk."

Peachie Fortune marched me out of the farmhouse and down the path past the barn to the cowshed. There was Brownie Belle where I left her munching on some hay in her manger.

Peachie Fortune stopped and told me, "Stroke her nose and hold her still while I search her tail."

"For what?" I asked.

"We kept the ones we could not find, but those we found we left behind," she recited. "The fairy tether, lass, is three twisted plaits put in a cow's tail by a good neighbor to play a prank on an old friend. Now hold that cow still. If I'm kicked, I'll take it ill."

I looked deep in Brownie Belle's two soft eyes, drinking in her sweet breath, the sweetest of any of us on Wicked Hill. While I was murmuring to her what a good cow she was, my eyes lit on some carving done with a penknife on the post above her stall.

"Here it is!" cried Peachie. She pulled three small blue feathers tied in scarlet thread twined three times inside the cow's tail. "Poor gal," said Peachie stroking the cow's side. "What a good little gal not kicking Peachie. You knew I meant no harm." She rubbed her hand over Brownie Belle's head. "You'll give milk now." She turned to me. "Give her a try."

I reached for the milk stool and grabbed the pail there in the hay. "What's that carved on the wall?" I asked.

"Why, I don't know. Let me see," said Peachie. "There's an O plain as day and there's a Y. And that first'un could be a D, so maybe that other is an R. Dory! Why, Dory must have done it afore she left."

"Dory?" I asked.

"Doris Sawyer was her name, but I always called her Dory. She said I was the only one to call that and here she must have carved it herself on the wall."

"She was the one afore me," I said. "The one who left at the spring thaws without saying good-bye."

"Maybe she did," said Peachie fingering the lettering carved in the barn wood.

Brownie Belle mooed, and the milk began to flow.

Once the pail was filled, we clamped on the lid and hurried back to the farmhouse where Miss Henrietta waited.

"About time!" she exclaimed as we entered the little backroom full of books. "Now, you, girl," she said to me, "find me a reaching stick, limber as a switch, and fetch it to the cookhouse." My lady turned to her cook. "Mistress Fortune, you come with me. We must stoke the stove in the cookhouse for this business to be done."

So we all left our separate ways, the women to the cookhouse and I out into the woods to find a switch. I thought of the switches my maw would send me to fetch, one for a good whipping. I got to be good over time at finding just the right kind of switch, one that stung but left no mark, yet gave a loud snap! Birch was best, I reckon, and there was a birch field out toward the windy side of Wicked Hill, only I dare not go where the poison ivy grows. Maybe if I circled round the hill I could reach the birch field from the other side.

I set off the road that wound up the hill from the farmhouse. It ended at a tilted bird bath, but from there twas only a short hike to the birch field where I would find a fine switch. There were plenty silver and white sticks on the ground. Somehow I knew that Miss Henrietta would want a brave, strong stick as stout as she was. I tested those I found by whipping the sticks through the air, leaning to see which would make a bow, feeling the grip for reaching.

While I searched for the right reaching stick, time must have passed until again I got that feeling that I was being watched. I froze, trying to figger out if it were man or beast. I listened, but heard no heavy breathing, so I whipped around looking left and right, then down. There! In a thicket of brush, within spitting distance, was that black cat called Tabitha. She stuck out a paw and showed her claws.

Our eyes met. Suddenly she leapt and I batted her with the stick, but she ducked in time and scratched my cheek. I dropped the stick when I felt blood. When I pulled away my hand, there was a streak of red in my palm.

I turned to run, only there she was again right in my way. The cat had landed on her feet and was crouched on her hind legs ready to spring. I ran back, but Tabitha followed in easy leaps. At a turn in the path, she leaped in front of me. I stagger back as she growled. As she paced steadily forward, the growl started low then began to build into a howl. I kept stumbling backward, as she snarled. She was stalking me, eye to eye, moving me back, step by step.

As we turned in this slow, queer little dance, I realized where the cat was taking me. Across the birch field and into the poison ivy! Where I was told not to go! What a mean old pussy! I hated her on sight since that first night—because I knew she hated me.

I broke out in a sweat waiting for the cat to strike again, but Tabitha must have moved me where she wanted, or else she was done playing cat and mouse. With a loud yowl she jumped over my shoulder and into the thicket while I could but crouch and wince. Only when I knew that the cat was gone and that I was safe, did I look up to see where I was.

There they were—stones with carvings all in a row across from the poison ivy. Each of them had writing on them. *Rose,* something, something, *Pearl,* something, something, *Grace,* something, something. Weren't those the names of the hired girls? These were headstones! I was in the graveyard of the hired girls who died on Wicked Hill.

CHAPTER V: THE SILVER PENNY

Medieval travelers believed that if they carried mugwort about with them, they would not tire on their journeys, and that those already weary could be cured either by drinking an eggshellful of the expressed juice, or by laying an ointment made from the leaves beaten in hog's lard upon their feet.
  —Christina Hole's *Encyclopedia of Superstitions*

When I got to the cookhouse, my lady and her cook were fast at work. Neither seemed to notice as I slipped in the door. Keeping my head down, I watched Mistress Fortune stoke the fire. She was the one who fed me my first night on Wicked Hill, and she was the one who found me a place to sleep at night. She also would have been the one to dig the graves for those other girls she fed and tucked in snug at night. I could not see either Miss Henrietta or Miss Marietta with a shovel.

Outside Miss Marietta was singing to the chickens, though by now we all blamed her for them not laying. I kept staring at Peachie Fortune. How it must harden a body year in year out always digging another grave! And just why had no hired girl stayed past the spring?

"Oh, you're back," said Miss Henrietta, turning around. "Bring here that reaching stick. Let me test it while the milk boils." She turned back to her cook. "Keep the saucepan filled, Mistress Fortune. The milk must boil over for the recipe to work."

I brought her the birch branch, which she flexed like a whip, while the fresh milk on the stove started to boil.

"Stand back, girl," my lady told me, "and watch how a pretty blood pudding is made."

With that, she turned and whipped the milk in the saucepan with the birch rod fetched for a reaching stick. Scalding milk was flung everywhere, but still Miss Henrietta struck the birch rod into the saucepan. The sight of gray smoke, the smell of burned milk, and the sounds of the stove fire crackling filled the cookhouse. I watched as the fresh white milk turned dark, then red in the saucepan. No more was the birch rod flinging milk, but blood on the cookhouse floor, while outside Miss Marietta was singing louder and louder.

Miss Marietta was not singing, she was screaming! Shrill cries of help sent us running up the path to the barnyard — me in front, Mistress Fortune right behind, and Miss Henrietta taking her time pulling up the rear.

When I reached the barnyard, there my lady sat under the tilted post that held the dinner bell, screaming loud and making faces. "Take them off, take them off. Boo-hoo! They hurt me so!" she cried kicking her feet. I rushed up and tried to untie the laces, but Miss Marietta kept kicking, until Mistress Fortune came and held her until I could get her kid boots off.

The first boot came off spilling blood, so did the other running a red stream down to puddle in the sand. My lady's white socks were pink when I peeled them off and her feet were raw and cut to ribbons. Each time I touched the boot tongue or removed a sock, Miss Marietta would scream even louder. Then Miss Henrietta would dip some more snuff and spit, ringing the dinner bell above her sister's head. Finally Miss Henrietta had laughed enough.

"Back to butter and eggs for us, and back to your cabin for you, Old Girl," she said walking away. She bent down and picked up the yellow bumbershoot. "I shall borrow this for a keepsake," Miss Henrietta said, "and you may keep the pin." She showed us all the back of her head as she heaved up the steps to her back porch. Out of nowhere, that black cat Tabitha sprang to the back step to follow her inside.

"Can you get to your feet?" I asked Miss Marietta.

"Of course not!" she snapped. "I cannot move my feet, let alone stand on them."

"Better get the wheelbarrow," Mistress Fortune told me, which is how I got Miss Marietta home.

I come up behind her with the wheelbarrow, and then Mistress Fortune and I together scooped her in. The cook left us for the path to the cookhouse, so it was up to me to get my lady down the path to the cabin. The way going down is steeper than going up. I had to go slow through the woods to the cabin, stopping often, and nearly dropping my lady twice. All the while Miss Marietta made a catawampus that I tried putting out of my mind.

Still, I could not help hearing some of the nonsense my lady spouted. How she would get even, how the next time she would have the whip hand, how once she found the right key, she would drive her sister off Wicked Hill. I let her rave until we got to the cabin door, and then she had to walk, or hobble anyways, to get inside. I had her favorite wicker chair set just inside the door. I plumped it with pillows and fetched the hassock. The kettle was still on the hearth, so I fixed her a cup of Dittany tea.

Once I had her settled, I went to the pitcher and filled the basin with water and Epsom salts she kept under the dry sink. While I let her feet soak, I took her little bottle of scent and dabbed her forehead until the crying stopped.

"You're a dear child," my lady said when finally calm.

I looked at the raw sores on both her feet. "I know a poultice Miss Juanita Jenkins taught me to make after she danced herself sore at a barn dance. You got any pig lard?" I asked.

For on the first day I climbed up Wicked Hill, I had seen from the footbridge a wild clump of blue brush that grew low on the hillside. This, I knew, was mugwort, that had many cures and uses. It was a remedy for palsy and a guard against lightning. With pig lard mugwort made a powerful poultice for easing foot sores and healing feet, and that is just what I set off to do.

I did not mind the long walk up the path and around the front and down the road to the footbridge. No one was about, just me alone with my thoughts running through my head like the moaning wind on Wicked Hill. The mugwort grew on the hillside where the wind blew the sharpest, above that all-devouring river with no name. I thought about the footbridge and how the wide world stood just on the other side, but I knew here I would stay, for I still had no place to go. Truly I did not much know where I was, other than on Wicked Hill. The devil you know is always better than the devil you don't. Those other hired girls must have made the same choice to their doom. All except maybe for Doris Sawyer, who seemed to have got out in time. At least I had seen no headstone starting with a D. Dory made it through the winter and still left before the spring thaws, so maybe I would too.

On the hillside I steadied myself as a wild wind whipped around. I almost slipped and would have fallen into that all-devouring river, but I grabbed hold of the bush of mugwort and it held. As I held on to those spindly blue stems, I heard church bells and knew what day it was. I had forgotten the Sabbath.

I remembered my church in Fool's Gap where Preacher Davey Snodgrass gave the message and Miss Juanita Jenkins played the pianee. I thought of my pretty little Polly dress that used to look so fetching on me. I could not stop feeling sorry for myself there with the lonesome wind wailing all around me and the very earth groaning under my feet.

Where the wind blew the sharpest, the groaning came the loudest. I wandered on around the bluff and saw where most of groaning was coming from. There in the rock side of the cliff was a long dark hole that dwindled away down under Wicked Hill. That's where the moaning come from—a sad, dying sound coming deep from within—and I remembered Mistress Fortune saying how one day that devouring river will bear all away, even Wicked Hill.

That sad sound lingered long within me as I trudged back to the cookhouse. I hoped Mistress Fortune was not about for I could not face her, not yet, knowing now what I knew.

The kitchen was empty. I went to the larder and found the can of pig lard, then took a rolling pin from the hanging rack and rolled the mugwort blooms like dough on a dish towel. Then I added the pig's lard, spreading it evenly among the mugwort with my fingers. I heard something stir behind me.

"Goodness, Amy! I did not mean to startle you," said Peachie Fortune coming through the Dutch door. "Why, look at you, girl, you're shivering!"

I could not face that old digger of young girls' graves, so I took the poultice and rushed past her with the sounds of "Amy! Annamay Scoggins!" ringing in my ears.

When I got the cabin, Miss Marietta was dozing in the wicker chair. The fire in the hearth had died, but I blew on the embers and soon got it going. In the meantime she woke.

"You're a good girl, you are," she told me happily enough, digging around for her bag of snuff. "Is that for me?" she asked, seeing the poultice.

I nodded and lifted her sore and ragged feet out of the pan of water and wiped them clean. Her knobby toes had rough, milky toenails looking like half moons. I nearly gagged at the thought of handling them.

Staring at her large horny toes, I was mindful of a sermon Reverend Davy Snodgrass gave on the washing of feet. How our Lord and Savior had set us all a good example by washing Peter's feet, even though Peter did not like it. Then I thought of Lazarus, the poor man with sore feet, who needed dogs to lick his sores, and here I was only dipping my hands in the pig lard and smearing mugwort on the crusty calluses of some old woman's toes. I sighed and set to work.

Miss Marietta began to coo as I rubbed her feet with the poultice and then wrapped them in the dish towel. All of a sudden Miss Marietta opened her eyes and cried, "Now you won't leave me here alone tonight! What if I need to get up?"

I did not relish sleeping with the cook in the cookhouse that night, but I also was not ready yet to just agree.

"I'll pay," she added," better than coppers," she said digging in her reticule.

"I thought you did not want me here while you're sleeping," I said.

"I don't want you watching me when I sleep," she said, then smiled. "But if you sleep, I don't mind watching you."

She held out her hand. "For you," she said. It was a silver penny.

"No thank you, ma'am," I said, "but I'll take a copper if you're offering."

I got my copper, so I spent the night, dozing in the wingback chair. Ever so often I could hear thunder and I would open my eyes to see the dark flicker with light.

"Heat lightning," Miss Marietta would say, staring straight at me with a smile.

"Awful late in the year," I might say, settling back in the chair.

Miss Marietta would nod, staring straight at me. "We get strange weather at odd times on Wicked Hill."

Then I would start to doze and dream, sometimes of the farmer with the white horse. On that long ride from the depot, he had told me odd things about Wicked Hill. One of the things he had said was whenever there's lightning, folks all around say that witches are warring on Wicked Hill.

Morning came with the cockcrow. Already it was light outside and I was late for my chores. I got up with a start.

There was Miss Marietta still smiling and staring at me. She was still wide awake when I brought her breakfast, no corn mush and molasses this day, but flapjacks with honey and butter and apple preserves.

Peachie Fortune did not scold when I rushed in the kitchen late, neither did I say a word to her. Pride probably kept her from speaking first and expecting no answer. Fear kept me silent. Who were these women and where had I found myself? The answer to that was clear enough. Wicked Hill!

We mostly went about our way wordlessly around each other until about midday, when Mistress Fortune stood in front of me as I headed for the door.

"So, Amy Scoggins, the cat got your tongue?"

I rubbed my cheek. "The cat scratched my face."

"Is that why you've been pouting? Silly girl!"

I rubbed the scratch with the back of my hand. "I may get the fever from a cat scratch, but at least that mean old tabby cared more for me than you. It's a sad state when a body cannot be trusted more than a cat!"

The old cook turned her hatchet face toward me. "Whatever can you mean?" she snapped.

I stared right at her. "I know why I am not to take the shortcut through the birch field. There's a graveyard in that poison ivy. That mean old cat showed me. She made sure that I knew about the other hired girls. That's more than you would do."

Mistress Fortune's eyes fell. She turned her head and no longer faced me. Then she sighed. "What's the point of warning you when you were already here?" She looked up at me. "I warned you about the silver penny."

"And I trusted you about the silver penny, but no more!"

Mistress Fortune looked grave. "Now see here, Amy, there's folks who know how to make a hoodoo. They spit on a silver penny to bring bad luck to whoever gets it. Touch not the silver penny."

"Did you tell every one of the girls you buried the selfsame thing?" I asked, and then showing her my back, I walked out the door.

Meanwhile Miss Marietta and I got on together famously, and I found that my chores were light if I stayed in the cabin. Mostly I was there to keep my lady company while she lay abed and played with her tray of rusty locks. She showed me their many parts—the cams and springs and bolts, plates and tumblers and pins—and how they fit together.

"Oh! There are all sorts of locks in this world," she told me. "There's a doorplate with a lock that stays fixed in a door and a padlock that can be moved about. There are combination locks and puzzle locks. Why, I heered tell of locks that can shoot bullets at burglars or slice off fingers of thieves, like that no good sister of mine, who locked me out of my own home." She still had a bellyful of bile toward her sister, but as long as her feet were sore there was nothing she could do but complain.

"I got her good once," she told me, "and I shall again! Ever heard of a booby trap, child?"

"That's where someone fills a pail of water," I said, "and perches it on a door left ajar."

My lady grinned and clapped hands, "So when the door opens, a booby gets wet!" She dipped her snuff and cackled. "Only it was not simple water that fell on my sister that day. It was that clock she still prizes that crashed on her head. It was the last time that clock rang the hour!" She laughed. In her merriment, she spat a wad of tobacky across the room to hiss and sizzle on the hearth. When her laughter finally used up all her breath, she sighed. "Of course, then I had to move out of my room in the farmhouse and live here."

"How come you let her?" I asked, wondering what could make someone give up a home with a room and a bed.

Miss Marietta wrinkled up her pert nose. "Just as there is a booby trap, so there is a booby prize. She made one and passed it on to me and I have had bad luck ever since."

"The silver penny?" I asked.

Miss Marietta's smile failed her. She looked sharp, scanning my face to see what I knew. "That's right, child, she passed me the silver penny. I was planning on offering it to you, but you are too wise to take it."

"That I am," said I.

"And too good a girl, I reckon," said Miss Marietta. "I would not have the heart to play such a dirty trick on someone so kind and obliging."

I could not help but smile. Miss Marietta had her whims, but perhaps I had found a kind mistress at last. "The poultice should heal your feet entirely in another day," I told her.

Miss Marietta smiled. "Tomorrow I shall walk again, and all because of you."

The next day I told Peachie Fortune what Miss Marietta said.

"So, you are speaking to me again, are you, Amy Scoggins?"

"There's naught else to do," I answered. "I know about the silver penny."

"Do you now!" said Mistress Fortune. "Perhaps you know how Miss Henrietta conjured her sister to take it. Do you think Miss Marietta simpler than you, that she knew naught about hoodoos and witch balls?"

I did not answer her and we fell into silence for the rest of the day.

Soon thereafter Brownie Belle wandered off her pasturage on a knoll beyond the cowshed. We went out looking for her on the windy side of Wicked Hill. At the tilted bird bath we stopped and looked over the rise. There below was a rock smokehouse, or so I thought. The walls had settled funny, so the front sunk lowered in the ground than the back. When we got around to the other side, instead of a door I saw a stone slab that had carvings. An angel with wings and curly hair put a finger up to his smiling face as he lifted his bare foot over the threshold of a door left ajar.

Mistress Fortune slapped her hand against the stone slab. "There's a fortune of treasure in there. Everybody knows it, but no one knows how to get it."

"In the smokehouse!" I cried, not meaning to speak at all, but in a smokehouse?

"It's the Wicks sepulcher," Peachie Fortune said. "My old Mam is interred therein. Look at the size of it, and fit for one person only. That's why it's believed a secret roomful of treasure is buried with her, only the tomb is sealed and no one can pry loose the stone."

I was not yet willing to be gulled into talking to the old traitor while I still had a grudge to pick. "Too bad there's no place in there for you," I said. "You will have to be stuck with the rest of us in the graveyard with the poison ivy."

Peachie Fortune frowned, then sighed. "The graves filled up slowly, Amy, over many years. Not all the hired girls who work here end up there. Some leave on their own two feet."

"Like who?" I asked.

"Like Dory," Peachie Fortune said attempting to smile. "Little Dory with the pretty yellow hair, she got away by the time of the spring floods. I know she did. She's long gone or I would know where she was."

"How come?" I said sullenly.

"Dory and I were close, that's why," she said. "I knew all about her dreams, how there was a boy she loved, only his folks disapproved, but when she made her fortune, she was going home, so he could marry her. I figger once she got home he would marry her anyway, fortune or no, all for her pretty yellow hair."

"So how did the others die?" I asked, almost afraid to know.

Mistress Fortune looked off in the distance as if remembering, then sighed again. "All died by natural ways, mostly. One died of fever, and one by a cold. One drowned trying to ford the river, and then one died by her own hand. After that I forget, or I just don't want to remember." Peachie Fortune shook her shoulders and wiped her brow with the back of hand. She squinted in the late afternoon light. "Look," she said, "there's the Guernsey by the crepe myrtle."

We got Brownie Belle and took her back to the cowshed, and then the cook went to the cookhouse and the hired girl to the cabin. Miss Marietta was standing up when I came through the door.

"I'm healed!" she told me clapping her hands. "Thanks to you, my girl, thanks to you. Let's celebrate! Pour me some wine. The decanter is on the sideboard."

"Wine the mocker?" I asked. I was quoting Proverbs 20, one of Preacher Snodgrass's favorite scriptures.

"Wine that maketh glad the heart," Miss Marietta said, quoting Psalms 104 back at me. "Pour one for yourself."

"Me, drink wine?" I said, agog at the notion.

"Drink up, Amy Scoggins," she said, using my name for the first time. "It's been a rare party these last three days, but now it must end. You must sleep in the cookhouse tonight. Have a glass before we say good night."

I thought maybe I could use something fortifying if I were to sleep under the same roof with that cook again. I went to the sideboard and found a cup on a little glass stem and poured the wine, which ran red into the cup. "Look not upon wine when it is red," I said, quoting, Proverbs 23, mostly to myself.

But my lady knew verse 31 and quoted like a Christian. "It biteth like a serpent and stingeth like an adder, but that's why we drink it, girl!"

I sniffed the glass. "Be not drunk with wine," I said, "Ephesians, Chapter 5, verse 18."

Miss Marietta shut one eye at me. "Give wine to those of a heavy heart," she said, "Proverbs 31: 6."

I thought with a heavy heart of having to go back to that cookhouse with that traitorous cook.

"Use a little wine for thy stomach's sake," Miss Marietta cooed. That was First Timothy Five, verse 23, and I guess she just outquoted me! So I took a swig and she chuckled as I downed it whole. All of a sudden I had the coughing fits.

My lady guffawed. "That's how we drink wine here on Wicked Hill!" she claimed. "Pour you another." And so I did.

The wine tickled down my throat and the room began to glow. How warm the fire in the hearth seemed! My head began to spin. Soon my lady was leading me by the hand.

"I'm so glad we come to know each other better," Miss Marietta told me at the door.

"Oh, so am I," I said. "I feel I have found a friend."

"God bless you, child," Miss Marietta said embracing me.

We hugged. That's when I felt something drop in my apron pocket. My head stopped spinning.

The cabin door was still ajar, so there was just enough light for me to see. I reached in and there in my palm was a silver penny. The silver penny I had been warned so not to take! It now rested in the palm of my hand while I stared dumbfounded, as Miss Marietta slammed the door behind me and locked it, casting me into the dark.

CHAPTER VI: STRANGE DREAMS

A dream out of season,
Trouble out of reason.
—2001 *Southern Superstitions*

That night came strange dreams. Now I don't usually dream. I am known for sleeping like a baby, nestling deep down in some sheltered place no matter what may hap around me; that is, before I came to Wicked Hill.

All that night I seemed to walk down some dark road with twisty corners and switchbacks. Or else, I seemed to be trudging upstairs and down, looking for something. I don't recall seeing a single solitary sight at all. I might have been in some unlit house at midnight. I seemed to spend the night opening windows, slamming doors, pulling drawers out and then in, and pacing floors.

I woke the next morning with swollen eyes and a black taste in my mouth. I had a hard time with my chores, so tired and sleepy I was for all of it being daylight. The sunlight hurt my eyes until my head ached. I thought myself the most miserable critter on Wicked Hill until I took the breakfast tray to Miss Henrietta in the farmhouse. When I entered the little backroom filled with books, she started suddenly from her chair. Her hair was a fright, all up in the back, like a haint! Her eyes were all wild and blood-shot, like a haint! When she saw who it was and why I was there, she settled back down and let me serve her.

"I've had a hard time," she told me. "Was there a storm last night on Wicked Hill?" she asked.

"I was dead to the world last night, Miss Henrietta," I told her.

She looked at me curious. "You wouldn't have heard the wind, then. It kept me up all night rattling the windows and slamming doors. I could hear it go up and down the stairs and rolling across the floors." She spread her arms to show me the room around us. "Look at the papers spread on the carpet. They seem to have flown straight out of the desk drawers, so the wind must have stirred them somehow."

I picked up the papers for Miss Henrietta and checked the doors and windows, then staggered back to the cookhouse, worn out with only the day half gone. I looked up the steps at my snug little pallet in the loft, but Peachie Fortune had dishes for me to wash, which meant priming the pump and then toting firewood to stoke the stove to boil water for dish washing. I was ready to plunge my hands into the scalding suds, when Peachie handed me the two wine glasses.

"How come two are dirty?" she asked and I told her. "You are too young and she too old for you both to be drinking wine together. I will not stand for it, Amy Scoggins. No hired girl under me will wind up a wine-bibber!"

I blushed to the roots of my curly red hair, shamed and fearful. Oh, what would my little church in Fool's Gap think! What would Preacher Davy Snodgrass say! I was so crestfallen at the cook's cold, hard words that I dast not tell of the silver penny still in my apron pocket.

The silver penny was stuck in a hard gray ball of goo, sticky as gum, slick as spit. My hand felt defiled just holding it, yet I could not help but reach for that lump of perdition ever so often just to see if it were still there. Later that day I begged Miss Marietta to take it back.

"Oh, no, my dear," she said sweetly, all smiles, "that is my little gift that I promised you."

"But you said I was too smart to take the silver penny."

"We seem both to be wrong," she said, her eyes all a twinkle. Then when I begged, she shushed me. "The only thing to do with a booby prize," she told me, "is to pass on the bad luck to someone else. I dare say Old Peachie who has fed me so straightly is due for some. Slip it to her, and then come tell me. There'll be another glass for you." I looked at the decanter on the sideboard and my mouth watered.

All that day the bad penny burned a hole in my pocket. I decided to hide it in the soft pine needles at the bend in the path leading to the barnyard. The dinner bell rang, and I felt a little easier than I had before, so I went for my supper and hoped for sweet dreams that evening.

That night no sweet dreams came. Instead, I dreamt I was buried alive, only my coffin was so large that I could wander around in it, banging on its peaked top to open it, and pounding on the gray padded sides and shouting for help. I woke ere cockcrow, wet with sweat and worn out from the night's passage.

I was not the only one worn out that next morning. When I fetched Miss Henrietta her breakfast tray, the old lady stared at me with heavy lids and deep shadows about her bloodshot eyes. "What a time I've had!" she cried. "Something has been rattling all night in the attic. I could hear it all the way down here. Go to the pantry, and under the sink drag out the traps. You go to the attic and set them immediately. And get the beaver trap. It's hanging from the rafter on the back porch."

"There can't be a beaver in your attic," I said, trying to reason with her.

"Do as I say," Miss Henrietta snapped. "There may be a rat somewhere in the house too big for the rat traps."

Of course, rats are just contrary enough to grow too big for rat traps. She had me there. I could not argue with that, so off I went and soon was trudging up the long stairs to the attic with my arms full of mice traps and rat traps, and dragging the beaver trap behind. The long hall upstairs goes the length of the downstairs hall then turns up a little stairwell by the sleeping porch. Three steps lead to a trapdoor that opens up to the floor of the attic above. This was my first time going to the attic and I did not relish the prospect. It proved just as dark and dusty as I expected, but the attic was also quiet and empty and as still as a tomb. Climbing up inside, I remembered my dream. I rapped on the pointed ceiling and felt the gray walls padded with newspaper to keep out the cold.

"What's that noise up there?" called Miss Henrietta from the bottom step. "Do you hear it? That's the same noise that kept me awake all night long!"

I set all the traps as I was bidden, but I left the attic not expecting any mice or rats at all.

When I walked down from the farmhouse, I passed by the pine tree in the bend of the path, only to stop and check on the silver penny I had buried among the soft needles underneath. I began to fret about leaving it there in the open, so I took it back in my pocket to find a better place to hide it away, but come nightfall the only place to put it was beneath my pillow.

That night I dreamed I was lost in the bottom of deep dark well, crying like a baby cries for its mama. All night long I wept, and cried, and screamed, and shouted for anger so that I woke by first light bone tired and weary of life altogether. I tired of pulling my socks up in the morning, I tired of Brownie Belle, and the Blue Hollands, and I tired mostly of that no-good cook watching me closely to catch me doing wrong. I staggered up the path from the cookhouse and on through the backdoor of the farmhouse with Miss Henrietta's tray.

There in the little backroom full of books, I must have woke her, even though the sun was already out. She came to with a start, raising a shotgun on her lap. Tabitha with a cry jumped for cover.

"Don't shoot!" I yelled, quivering so hard the china rattled.

Miss Henrietta lowered the gun. "Oh, so it's you. Someone's in the cellar! All night long I stayed here hanging on to Old Betsy with my finger on her trigger too scared to move."

"Perhaps it's just the rats you heard the other night," I said.

"Do rats shout and scream and weep and cry?" she asked.

Miss Henrietta had me there again, for, no, rats do many ornery things, but never have I heard them shout or scream or weep or cry. Still, I did not relish traipsing down into her dark, dank cellar, especially if some madman was unhappy to be down there.

"Bring your gun," I said, "and come with me, for I'm not going down there alone."

Miss Henrietta was about to fuss, but she saw in my eye that I weren't fooling and nor could she blame me. She rose with my help. I gingerly took the gun by the barrel and pointed it away from both of us in case it went off. The cat, I didn't care about.

My lady shrugged her shoulders and shook her gray curls and pulled her knit shawl tight around her. We marched down the long hallway to a little panel door under the staircase that led to the root cellar. With one hand I held an oil lamp and with the other Old Betsy while Miss Henrietta stayed on the top stair just to keep me company. Each step led me down into the musty dark that smelled of earth and water and stone, but nothing else—no rats, no man. At the bottom of the steps I reached out my arm and shone the lamplight into the left corner, then into the right. Then I whipped around sudden-like and did the same in the two corners behind me. Nothing! My lady could not believe that her cellar was empty.

"I tell you what I heard," she insisted, no longer afraid, only peeved, as she peered down the steps of the root cellar to check for herself.

"Shine the light over there," she would say, "or try over here," until finally she gave up hoping to find the madman who scared her all night.

"Three nights in a row," she groused. "Three nights!"

I nodded.

"You too?" she asked, for the first time interested.

We had climbed back out of the root cellar and were standing in the front hall, not knowing what to do next. That's when we heard Miss Marietta out on a stroll. She was much stronger now that her feet had healed. She was in high color and in fine fettle, unlike her sister who stood so pale and drawn.

"Funny how both of us would suffer so on the same nights," 'Miss Henrietta observed.

Just then Miss Marietta took off singing. She warbled this sad little song, "I Dreamt I Dwelt in Marble Halls." Oh, what a sweet, sad little song it was! It tugged at my heart to hear about those halls where there were rubies and slaves, but not the one she sang to.

"That's it! That's it!" cried Miss Henrietta. "I'll put a stop to this foolishness here and now." With that, my lady stormed into the little backroom full of books and brought back Miss Marietta's yellow parasol.

"I need that yellow cigar box on the bureau in the best bedroom. Fetch it, girl."

When I brought the cigar box to Miss Henrietta, she called out the backdoor. "Oh, sister dear!" Miss Henrietta cried. "Please sing us just one more chorus, please."

Miss Marietta started up again a trilling as Miss Henrietta took from the box three red skeins of thread. "Three threads of red twined three times three," she chanted as she wound the red tassel around the yellow parasol. "Three threads of red wound three times three," she said a second time. Then, "Three threads of red wound three times three." The great fat tower of a woman stared at her work there in her hands, then took a deep breath. "Once, twice, thrice!" she counted and took the yellow parasol and broke it over her knee.

Outside came a loud whoop. Miss Marietta had taken a spill. Her back was out. I ran to fetch the wheelbarrow as her sister came out to enjoy the fun. How Miss Henrietta laughed, a deep-throated ugly chortle, as her sister cried each time I tried to scoop her up.

"My back! My back!" she cried, and Miss Henrietta just laughed. She laughed so hard that her laughter turned to coughing.

When I finally got Miss Marietta into the wheelbarrow, I looked around to see Miss Henrietta all red in the face and gasping. She was choking!

I rushed up and started slapping her hard between the shoulders until she coughed up what was bothering her and spat on the ground. I gazed in wonder at the little steel pin come from nowhere, back in the same place where I found it first in the barnyard sand. As Miss Henrietta caught her breath, now her sister Miss Marietta, no longer crying, set off a laughing herself, and another day on Wicked Hill had begun.

CHAPTER VII: THE STAR KEY

Certain songs and airs are considered by musicians to be very unlucky. 'I Dreamt that I Dwelt in Marble Halls' is so ill-omened that even to hum it without thinking may bring serious misfortune.

—Christina Hole

Once Miss Marietta was laid up with a backache, then stopped the bumps in the night up at the farmhouse. Also, my nightmares stopped, but still I dreamed. These dreams, though, were restful now, always in a warm sunshine, walking with Miss Marietta in my dreams; we always wandered in my dreams toward the windy side of Wicked Hill. There the wind blew through my head like a song... like the song Miss Marietta sang, "I Dreamt I Dwelt in Marble Halls." And Miss Marietta always walked before me, talking away about cams and springs and bolts, plates and tumblers and pins.

Then on the night of the full moon, I dreamed that I was all alone out on the windy side of Wicked Hill just above the Wicks Sepulcher. I walked around and around the tomb by moonlight looking in every nook and cranny, feeling for mortises and rims. "Cams and springs and bolts, plates and tumblers and pins," I sang to myself in my dream in the moonlight as the all-devouring river raged below. Then my finger found a little hole, which I had been searching for all the time without knowing why. Perhaps a keyhole, I thought, squinting at it in the moonlight. It might be no more than a carving. There were plenty around the tomb, but this was the only carving that I could find on the back wall. The carving was shaped like a star.

"The star key," a voice said in my ear.

In my dream I wondered, "What's that?" and the voice replied, "No matter, my love, come to bed. You've wandered long enough in the dark." That's when I woke up bitter cold on my little pallet with my feet damp as the morning dew.

The next day nobody spoke to me. Miss Marietta was in a sulk and spent all day in bed, while Miss Henrietta pored over her books and her ciphering not caring if I came or went. Mistress Fortune and I had few words for each other and it seemed more polite not to say anything at all. A quick nod or gesture was enough for us both these days, so one day no one spoke one word the whole day long. I went to bed worried that night. What if this be the beginning of how it's going to be all winter, or all life long? That couldn't be! Yet I went to bed troubled and tried to sleep. In my sleep, I dreamed.

I dreamed I was swinging on a door, like the sweep door to the dining room from the pantry, only the door I swung on must have been the front door next to the hat rack. I could tell the front door by its big brass lock I could see about eye level. There was the bright yaller square with the darkened keyhole in the center.

As I stared in my dream, a long white boney finger wormed its way out the keyhole. It beckoned me closer, like a white snake I saw once trap a baby bird, by the way it wiggled back and forth, back and forth, until I leaned forward and that blind finger shot forward and grabbed me by the nose!

The finger pulled me forward toward the dark center of the keyhole where I peered in and saw another eye staring back on the other side. This pale, cloudy blue eye blinked, and I heard a voice say, "How you toss and turn, girl! Lie back. Sleep," it chuckled, "and let me in."

Soon enough I was back in the warm sunshine with Miss Marietta happy as children holding hands as we sneaked through the farmhouse. "There are keys on the hat rack next to the front door," Miss Marietta told me. "Check them all."

"What are all these keys for?" I asked.

My lady shook her silver curls and pulled out her lorgnette. "There's one for the front door. That one's a skeleton key. It can open the front door or the back. And this one is for the pie safe in the pantry, and that one is for the piano in the front room. And this one is for the busted clock on the library mantel. Let's see this key," she said.

We floated into the front room where the pianee sat across from the clock on the mantel. Miss Marietta turned the clock around to show where the back was busted. "I did that," she gloated. "My sister can take many things away from me, but she can't take that."

"What are we looking for?" I asked.

"Check the sideboard. There was a key in the drawer, remember?"

The sideboard was in the dining room just behind the front room. Two big doors join the two rooms. In my dream the two doors swung open allowing us to pass. We floated by the sweep door to the sideboard where I jerked open the drawer. There among the linens was the key.

"Is it the star key?" she asked.

I looked at the key. "How can I tell?" I wondered.

But Miss Marietta pulled me along into the little backroom full of books. "Check the desk drawers."

I pulled out drawers and scattered papers just as I seem to remember doing before. In a little secret door that opened by a spring, we found a ring of old keys.

"Is it the star key?"

"How can I tell?" I asked.

"Bring them along," she said in my dream.

We drifted into the best bedroom across the hall. There Miss Henrietta snored with the cat Tabitha at the foot of the bed, staring at us. Miss Marietta looked at her sister sleeping.

"He would not have given her the secret. He built the outside, but did not know what was within. I ran him off before he found out."

"Found out what?" I asked.

"He knew about the star key. He must, since he carved the keyhole. But he did not know about the gold."

"What gold?"

"Come, child," Miss Marietta said in my dream, and we floated up the long stairs in the hallway.

We passed through every room using the skeleton key from the hat rack or else the ring of keys from the desk drawer. At the top of the stairs was the loom room, but there was no loom there, only two spinning wheels in front of each of the windows, one facing north, and one facing east. The old cedar chest at the other end of the room had a lock. A little key tied with a ribbon unlocked it. We looked through every quilt in it. "This quilt has the Martha Washington Flower Garden pattern," Miss Marietta said. "It's much too fine for use. Look, this is the friendship quilt my mother's friends made for her when she married. And here's the red checkered counterpane that her mother made who carded wool for the batting." There was one with two golden circles filled with flowers. "This is the wedding ring quilt I made one summer," she said, stroking it before setting it by.

Once we locked up the cedar chest we drifted across the hall to the upstairs guest bedroom. There was a big bed with curtains and a marble washstand and marble dresser. Both the mirrors in the washstand and in the dresser were gone. The cabinet beneath the washstand was empty, but the marble dresser had eight drawers and every drawer had a lock. And every key on the key ring was tried. Every key fit every keyhole, but there was no star key.

"We must consult the book of recipes," Miss Marietta said before leaving the upstairs. The sleeping porch in the back had a trapdoor that led to the pantry. In the pantry was where Miss Henrietta left the book with the speckled leather binding. There in the moonlight stood Miss Mariettta bent over its frayed pages muttering.

"Moonwort," was the last thing I remembered when I woke the next day.

CHAPTER VIII: MOONWORT

Woodpeckers apparently knew of the moonwort's power as well as human beings. Tradition has it that if they found any nail obstructing their nests, they laid moonwort leaves against it, and so drew it forth without difficulty.
–Christina Hole

Miss Marietta knew a lot about birds. "If you see a bluebird one day, there will be a fair day the next. A robin is a sure sign of spring. If a bobwhite only says Bob, then that means rain. If a chicken cock crows ten times, that is a sure sign of rain." I heard it all. When Marietta felt well enough to leave her sickbed, she began to follow birdsongs. She would take me out for long rambles through the woods on the back side of Wicked Hill.

"Look for a woodpecker, dear," she told me. "One woke me up this morning. It must be down here somewhere."

On she led me down the back of Wicked Hill where the pine trees grow thickest, and, though the middle of the afternoon, all was gloom. Dappled sunlight would dazzle me on rocks as I passed through into cool darkness on the other side. White dust motes danced in my eyes as Miss Marietta led me onward.

She stopped. "Listen! Do you hear?"

And off we would go down toward the marshes by that all-devouring river. Here that riling river swamped the low land where some scrub pines stood in the water with ferns all around. Down the back side of the hill we came upon sunshine once again and I could see straight once more.

There! Out of the blue, a little red-capped woodpecker landed on a dead branch of a hollow tree. Just above the branch was a hole in the hollow tree that the bird hopped into, carrying a bug in its beak. A moment later the little red-capped woodpecker hopped out and flew away.

Miss Marietta clapped her hands. "Hurry now," my lady told me. "Gather a mud pie from the mire around us and clog the woodpecker hole before it returns."

"And kill the little ones inside!" I cried.

"Hush, child. No nestling will be harmed. The bird will care for them better than that. You'll see. Now do as you're told!" She cuffed me on the ear and I ran off to the low spot where water bubbled up and the mud was easy to mold.

I got me a dirt clog and climbed up to the dead branch in the hollow tree and smeared the mud over the hole, careful not to let any mire fall inside the nest. When I had finished my fool's errand, I jumped down to the ground and Miss Marietta called me over to her.

"Now watch," she said.

Soon came the red-capped woodpecker back to the dead branch on the hollow tree. When she saw the hole was plugged, the mother squawked and then shot off over the marsh.

"Follow it!" Miss Marietta cried, taking off after the birdie. "Don't let it out of your sight!"

I picked up my skirts and lit out after the little red-capped woodpecker, almost losing my clogs in the chase. The little bird did not go far. It swooped down amidst the ferns that grew among the scrub pines. Then plucking one fern from the many, that little red-capped woodpecker headed back for home.

"You see the exact spot where the bird landed?" my lady asked, pointing at the ferns among the scrub pines. "Stand on that exact spot."

The scum water was knee deep where the ferns grew, but I did as I was told and she joined me there. We watched the red-capped woodpecker return to the dead branch on the hollow tree. With the sprig of fern in its beak, it touched the fern's tip to the dirt clog and dirt clog was gone! The dirt clog simply fell out from the hole like a star from the sky.

I looked at Miss Marietta in wonderment.

"Moonwort," she told me. "It has amazing properties. According to the book of recipes, it cleans pipes and unclogs drains and is reputed to open any lock. All I need is but a single frond of moonwort and we can forget the star key." Miss Marietta opened her mouth to tell me more, but the mouth itself reared back in surprise.

What does she see? I wondered.

I turned my head to see what my lady saw, and it was that black cat Tabitha getting read to spring. Tabitha, who tiptoed along the rocks of Wicked Hill without getting a paw wet, was stalking her prey, and now she sprung, jumping me from behind.

With a whoop, I beat her back with my waving hands, but she landed on my face anyway and clung to my forehead.

"Shoo! Shoo!" Miss Marietta cried and started to bat the cat off me.

Tabitha turned on Miss Marietta, spitting and twisting in my hair. I made to grab her sides. No soap. With a leap she landed on Miss Marietta's head and was now Miss Marietta's worry. So I began swatting the cat.

As we tussled, our skirts became heavy with water and threatened to swamp us, while our hands busily slapped about our heads. Every time we made a grab for the beast, a paw would shoot out and slap us down. Finally we both took off wading for dry land, which was all the cat was waiting for. It disappeared once we reached the hillside.

Miss Marietta turned around.

"Do you see her?" I asked, afraid Tabitha would strike once more.

Miss Marietta peered into the gloom. "No, I'm looking for the moonwort. Where was it exactly among all those ferns?"

I turned around and saw how many ferns there were all beaten down in the wide swath we made in our wake.

Miss Marietta stood there in the late afternoon light, counting. "Gather me three plants a day, starting today, and bring them by around sunset. I'm thinking about planting ferns around the Wicks sepulcher," she said.

CHAPTER IX: THE WITCH BALL

A witch can kill a person with a witch ball, which is made by rolling a small bunch of hair into a hard, round ball.
—2001 *Southern Superstitions*

W hen I finished my new chores, and nary a word about an extra copper for doing them, I hurried back to the farmhouse. I knew Miss Henrietta would scold me for being late. I would always stay and wait on her awhile before supper. Up through the backdoor left ajar, I rushed into the little back room filled with books, looking like a haint! Not that Miss Henrietta would notice. She had moved the busted clock from the front room mantel and was tinkering with its innards.

As I set about my work as noiseless as a spider, my lady was forever muttering about arcs and pivots and pendulums, bobs and sash weights and flywheels. Finally she looked up and stared right me as I cleaned the hearth to lay the fire.

"Girl, what happened to you?" she cried. "You look like a haint!"

Your cat just rubbed her claws through my hair, I should have said, but I thought better of it and stayed still.

"Girl, you look rode hard and put up wet," she claimed. "Better go into the best bedroom and fetch me my silver brush. It's next to the cigar box on the dresser."

Soon she had the heavy brush of tarnished silver with the big W carved in its back. She bade me sit down on the footstool next to the hearth. When I did, she reached around and began to brush my hair.

"What nice, thick, healthy hair you have here," she told me, brushing away. "So curly too."

I smirked. "Preacher Davy Snodgrass calls it my crown of glory. He once said that the angels in heaven will be hard pressed to give me a nicer crown that what's growing on my head."

"That Preacher Davy sounds sweet on you," said Miss Henrietta, brushing away.

I sighed. "He and I grew up together and played all the time when we were young'ns. It wasn't until his folks died of the fever that he took to preaching." I considered the matter as Miss Henrietta brushed my hair harder so my whole head tingled.

"What's this Davy Snodgrass look like?" she asked.

"Much like his namesake in scripture," I answered, "curly-headed and ruddy of countenance." I frowned. "Some people crumble when faced with death and loss, but Preacher Snodgrass has been strong in the Lord, whatever the hardship. He and Miss Juanita Jenkins were the mainstays of our little church in Fool's Gap once the fever took hold."

Miss Henrietta kept brushing. "Is the fever what run you off from home?" she asked.

I thought a moment on how I got to Wicked Hill. "No'm," I answered. "Miss Juanita Jenkins died, and so I left."

"And now you are here," she said, stopping her brushing. "All better!"

So I was. So I was! I left the farmhouse feeling a lot better. It was first time I had felt a gentle touch since I left home.

That evening after dinner and the dishes, Peachie Fortune and I slowly got ready for bed. I was drying my socks that got wet in the swamp and Peachie was combing her hair. Long and black it was without a gray hair to be seen. "It's cause I comb it out a hundred strokes each night," she told me.

I looked up at the clock on the hearth to see the time and remembered where I had seen that clock before. "That's the same clock that's in the farmhouse," say I.

"That or its twin," said Peachie Fortune.

"The one in the farmhouse don't work. It's broke," I said.

"That's because it belongs to Miss Henrietta. This one belongs to Miss Marietta. Only she swore she would never touch it again. There were these two clocks, you see. Both belonged to a peddler man, Abel Pratt with wavy brown hair. He was the one who carved the angel and the writing on the tomb."

"His are the tools left in the workshop?" I asked.

"That's the one. Oh, he was quite the darling one summer. Ezra Cain was the farm hand, and he and I used to talk about how the ladies in the farmhouse took on after pretty Abel Pratt. That was when the dining room was still used, and he always ate there with the ladies, seldom in the cookhouse with us. Pretty Abel Pratt had a careful way of talking. He would pay court through riddles."

"Riddles?"

Peachie Fortune nodded darkly. "What do judges keep, and sailors lose, parents fear, but lovers choose." She stared at me until I saw she meant me to answer, but I could only shrug.

"Court-ship. Get it?"

I wrinkled my forehead and thought. "What judges keep—court! And sailors lose, a ship? Parents fear but lovers choose..."

"Courtship!" we both cried together.

"Here's another one he pulled," the cook said. "What flowers does every lover find in a garden?"

I shook my head.

"Tulips," she answered.

"Oh, two lips." I laughed.

"Laugh you may," Mistress Fortune replied, "it was fair funny how the riddles worked on the sisters. Their way of reply was with flowers. Pansies at his breakfast plate, daisies on the doorstep, a red rose on his pillow at night. They swapped flowers among the three of them until one day Miss Marietta got a yellow chrysanthemum, and then there was hell to pay! You know the language of flowers, girl?"

I sat there looking stupid, so she sighed and went on with her story.

"Abel stayed through harvest and helped Ezra build the sepulcher, and this peddler man had these two mantel clocks in his pack that he wanted to sell. Miss Marietta, hoping for his favor, bought one for her hope chest, only to discover that he gave the other one to Miss Henrietta for free."

"So Miss Marietta broke Miss Henrietta's clock!"

"The two sisters have never sat down to eat together since," said Peachie, combing her hair. "Ninety-eight, ninety-nine, hundred. There!" She stopped combing and began plucking hairs from her comb to cast into the fire. They sparked and sizzled in the firelight.

"Why do you burn the stray strands?" I asked.

"So I know where they are," Peachie said. She started to plait her hair into a braid. "If you want to keep your hair like mine when you get my age, start combing it now, a hundred strokes each night."

"Miss Henrietta already brushed my hair today," I told her.

"She did?" Peachie let the plait go out of her hand. "You didn't think to clean the brush afterwards, did you?"

"No," I looked up surprised at the notion. "She didn't tell me to."

Peachie rose. "Get up! You cannot leave your stray hairs in that house overnight."

I glanced out the window. "But it's dark out! What if she's in bed? What would I say?"

"Say you come for your hairs," Peachie told me, grabbing my arm. "She'll not stop you if you tell her true."

She opened the kitchen door and pushed me barefoot into the night. "Don't come back without those hairs," were her last words to me as she shut the door.

It was night out, but not so dark that I could not see my way up the path to the farmhouse. The way back might be a different story though. I hurried on through the trees, wondering what I would say when I got to the door.

The backdoor was unlocked when I reached to the back porch and the lamp still burned in the long hallway. I slipped in without knocking. In for a penny, in for a pound, as Miss Juanita Jenkins would say.

The house was quiet and still. So far, so good.

First I checked the little backroom full of books. That's where Miss Henrietta combed my hair and she might have left the hairbrush there. The room was dim and ghostly, but empty. By the light of the banked hearth fire, I slipped about looking for the hairbrush, which was nowhere to be found. Then I remembered the cigar box that stayed on the mantel in the best bedroom where Miss Henrietta slept.

I shuddered at the thought of entering that room where no doubt she was, perhaps fingering the trigger of Old Betsy while listening to my footsteps. Still there was nothing for it, but to do it.

The door to the bedroom was shut. I had my hand on the knob ready to turn when I heard up the hall this loud flapping sound, like the wings of a mighty bird straining to take flight. What on earth? I listened to make sure I heard what I heard, and sure enough—flap, flap, flap!

The sound was coming from the little side room next to the front door. Did Miss Henrietta have an eagle trapped now? Could it be some haint with leathern wings?

Flap, flap, flap!

Whether haint or vicious bird of prey, I druther face either than wake Miss Henrietta with me in the house unbidden. Up the hall I hurried as softly as I could with just the light from the hall lamp to guide me.

That little room off the hall was mostly empty and served little purpose as I could tell. It had a sour smell and zig-zaggedy wallpaper that was peeling off at the top, no doubt from the dankness. I usually left a window open to air out the room. In fact, when I crossed the open threshold I could feel a breeze coming from the window I forgot to shut.

Flap, flap, flap! I wheeled around to face what was coming. Only there in the moonlight streaming through the open window, the room seemed as empty as ever. Just me and the moonlight shining in the corner where the wallpaper had come undone.

A wind came up and a breeze blew by me straight toward that corner of the room. Flap, flap, flap went the hanging piece of wallpaper. Smirking at my own foolish fears, I slipped over to the window to shut it before the wallpaper could be stirred by the air once more. I closed the window and breathed a sigh of relief to hear the great house silent again. That's when the hall lamp went out.

Was someone there? I stood stock still listening once more. Out in the farther reaches of the still house I could hear something, though not something moving on the ground. It seemed like a flapping sound once more, only this time not like a great winged creature trying to get airborne, but more like a little skittery, twittery critter already taken flight.

A bat! Of course, a house like this would have a bat. I had enough. I turned back to pry open the window once more and slide out to safety, even if it meant a drop onto the prickly bushes below. Only this time the window would not open. I tugged and tugged, but the window now was jammed. All the while the twittery, skittery sound came closer and closer. Then it dawned on me. How had I found myself cornered in the room farthest away from the backdoor and safety?

I squared my shoulders. It was only a bat, I told myself. I knew how to handle bats. I could untie my apron and throw it over the critter as it flew toward me to be hauled outside. Only I feared that the noise I would make might wake my lady.

There in the moonlight I saw a shadow and heard a swoop as something careened through the open threshold of the room. I stood stock still once more listening, wondering where that bat could be, all the while worrying somehow that it might fly right into my pretty curly hair.

I edged toward the threshold and slipped into the hallway once more. The front door was there at my elbow, so tried it, knowing it was locked. The key usually hung on a ribbon from the hall rack. As I fumbled for the ribbon, I felt like I was being watched, though how in the gloom and by whom I did not stop to consider. Instead I let go of the ribbon and eased along the wall toward the open double doors of the front parlor next to the stairs. As I did, I thought I could hear footsteps softly following.

Once inside the front parlor I found myself in complete darkness, darkness that covered me like soot. I stood once more unable to move, listening to what seemed to be careful silent treads moving toward the parlor doors. What could it be? Who could it be? Miss Henrietta was too stout to move so softly.

Though I could see nothing, I had cleaned that front parlor often enough to know my way around. I slipped past the big square pianee and avoided the horsehair settee. As I brushed past the what-not cabinet with the chalk fruit and china dogs, I definitely heard something move into the room, no longer caring to be so quiet as before. No matter, I was already at the dining room doors, which I slid through and shut.

I put my head to the door to listen and heard what seemed to be a sigh. Or was it the wind? I listened harder and could barely hear what seemed to be a wee little whisper. "Heh... heh," it hissed.

"I come for my hair!" I cried.

The noise I made emboldened whatever was there. I could hear the sounds of some giant wind sweeping around the parlor walls, thrashing about as if gnashing its teeth. I wondered that Miss Henrietta asleep in her best bedroom did not hear it, if indeed she had ever been there. Then I thought of the bat that had come out of nowhere, like the footfalls in the hallway, neither of which I had actually seen. Could all that I thought I heard — the bat, the steps, the wind, the voice — all be in my head?

Just then the doorknobs jiggled, so I ran. Across the dining room, through the sweep door, into the pantry and on to the kitchen, I hurried to the backdoor, but the backdoor now was locked! As I turned the deadbolt, I could hear something man-sized staggering blindly down the dark hallway. I flung open the backdoor and pushed against the screen door, only to find the screen door now had been latched as well!

I tugged at the latch as those shambling footsteps down the hallway kicked up a racket getting closer and closer, but the latch was stuck! I yanked and tugged at the latch, afraid to look back, knowing my only safety was not seeing for sure what it was coming after me. Only when I felt a hot breath on the back of my neck did the little hook on the backdoor pop out of its eyelet and I rushed outside, away from the house and its clutches.

Once outdoors, I knew I would not be followed. Whatever was of the house would stay there. I came away empty-handed, but still in my own skin. Without looking back, I beat my way once more across the moonlit sand of the hen yard and into the safe and sheltering night.

CHAPTER X: THE WICKS GOLD

Christmas Eve, and twelve of the clock,
Now they are all on their knees
                    —Thomas Hardy, *The Oxen*

That night I dreamt strange dreams. This time instead of walking with Miss Marietta all night, I spent all night with her sister, Miss Henrietta, who was forever telling me what to do.

In my dream we were back in her little room filled with books bending over her work table where stood the broken clock.

"In between the main wheel, the ratchet wheel, the flywheel and the escape wheel runs the barrel to the escapement," she would say.

"Coil the driving weight around the barrel and wind it around the ratchet wheel," she told me. "Attach the gong ratchet between the ratchet wheel and the main wheel."

I would stare at all the cogs and wheels not knowing which to pick up first.

"Turn the main wheel to set the arm to the escapement."

"What arm?" I cried.

"The main wheel turns the center wheel which turns the minute hand," she would say, as if reciting something committed to memory.

"The center wheel turns the flywheel, which turns the escape wheel, which turns the three-legged spindle by the chain where hangs the pendulum. Set the main wheel turning, and the center wheel turning, and the flywheel wheel turning to set the escapement."

"But how do I set the wheels a-turning?" I cried out in my dream.

"Pull the pendulum" came the answer.

I woke up tired at cockcrow, and when I got up off my pallet, I swooned. Back on the feather tick I lay listening to the second cockcrow before I could rise.

The rest of that long day was spent trying to catch up from sleeping in. Brownie Belle was mooing loudly for me to milk her by the time I reached the cowshed. Some of the Blue Hollands had wandered off by the time I got to feed them, and I had to chase them back toward the coop. Miss Henrietta had many things for me to do (no more talk of a copper for the extra work). Then in the afternoon I had to dig up ferns for Miss Marietta. Ever the silver penny burned a hole in my pocket. I buried it in the soft mud beneath the woodpecker hole, but I dug it up before nightfall.

My days became busy with nothing but work, working Miss Henrietta's will by day and Miss Marietta's will by night. Every night Miss Marietta would come to me in my dreams and we would still search for the star key. Every morning Miss Henrietta had a new chore for me to do.

Monday was washing day. I would pump water into copper pots to boil over the stove and then pour the boiling water into the big galvanized tub. There with the washboard and a bar of lye soap, I would wash the clothes, and sheets, and towels first thing so some might dry by evening. Then I would take the hot soapy water in buckets and scald inside the outhouse with a brush and a mop. By evening after serving Miss Henrietta, then Miss Marietta, and then again Mistress Fortune, I must iron and fold the laundry that was dry. What was left still damp by nightfall I must set on little wooden frames in the loft, and I would go to sleep with the smell of lye.

Tuesday was cleaning the dining room, where nobody ate. I took lemon wax kept in the sideboard and polished the oak table and eight chairs. Then I polished the sideboard and the standing silver chest by the window. Once I was done polishing wood, I set to polishing silver. All the silver knives and silver spoons and silver forks I polished until my hands turned red from the baking soda.

Wednesday was upstairs. All the bedrooms had to be cleaned once a week, whether anyone slept there or not. Each room had to be aired. The window raised and the bed remade. Each room had to be dusted and swept, including the sleeping porch over the pantry.

Thursday was trash day. Starting at the farmhouse I would empty the rooms of rubbish and then go to the cabin and do the same. Then I did the same for the cookhouse too. All the trash I stacked out behind the cookhouse and lit a fire. Every Thursday evening the four of us would gather round the fire, not so much for each other's company as for the sake of the fire. We would watch silently until the embers glowed late into the night and then go to bed.

Friday was the kitchen day. I started early scrubbing the sinks and boards and tables before sweeping and mopping the floors. Peachie Fortune and I would clean out the cabinets and wipe the shelves of the larder, keeping track of what we had and what we needed.

Saturday was baking day. I would help Peachie with the cookies and the sweetbreads we would eat through next week. Then Peachie always baked a cake for that next day. The next day was always Sunday, though no one mentioned the word. There was always cake on account of it being Sunday, though no thanks were given. All day I would listen with my ear half-cocked until I heard church bells off somewhere, and then I would always rest easy on my broom. I would get to be a little hopeful, only to have strange dreams that night and wake with the same week to start again.

Then one morning we woke to little white handkerchiefs put in all the windows, and we knew our old friend Jack Frost had visited. The weather turned cold and we were wearing sweaters now. That day Miss Henrietta rang the dinner bell in the barnyard for a moot.

The two sisters never ate together or visited each other, but every so often they had something to discuss, so someone would ring the dinner bell and we all would come a running. "We must turn our attention to the orchard and harvest the rest of the fruit," Miss Henrietta told us. "Everyone gather baskets and meet me under the apples trees."

Soon we were down the slope from the cowshed picking up the dark russets and bright snows, and the yellow delicious. We made three piles, those meant for eating, those meant for cooking, those meant for cider. There was a cider press in a room off the workshop in the barn. Peachie Fortune would feed the mouth of the press as I pulled the crank and pure apple squeezing dripped through the cheese cloth. Some would be made into cider, some into vinegar.

Apples meant for eating mostly went to the cabin or the farmhouse. Miss Marietta liked to hang the red russets by their stems in the back room of the cabin. Miss Henrietta liked a big bushel basket of yellow delicious for the backroom full of books.

Mistress Fortune took the pile meant for cooking. We made six barrels of applesauce to store in the cellar until next year. With the rest we made apple butter, and what did not make good apple butter we pickled into apple relish.

After that first cold snap, Mistress Fortune told me it was time to make lye.

Lye being needed both for soft soap and hard, we had to make it ourselves. There was the leach-barrel made of birch wood outside the cookhouse that we filled with grease from the cooking can and with ashes from the fireplace. This barrel the cook and I wrangled over to a set of stones near the well sweep. There we took turns pouring well water into the leach barrel until the lye ran out through a hole at the bottom into a galvanized tub.

I mostly poured the water from the well sweep into the leach barrel while Mistress Fortune built a fire nearby. If the lye in the tub was not thick enough to bear up an egg from the henhouse, then more ashes had to be poured in the leach barrel and the whole weary work started over again.

Finally when the lye would bear up an egg properly, we hoisted the galvanized tub, one on each side— careful not to spill any on us—over to the fire to let it boil into soap. Mistress Fortune used a sassafras stick to stir the mixture just like my maw did. It took twice twelve bushel baskets of ashes to make one barrel of soap, and there were two barrels needed for the next year.

"One barrel was the hard soap for washing clothes and scrubbing floors; t'other was the soft soap, clear as jelly, for the body and the hair," the cook told me.

"Strange to say," said I, "how something so needful and helpful to the body as soap could be so hurtful and burning as lye."

Then Peachie would say, "That's the way of things. The same fire that hardens clay melts wax. Many a year I have had to make lye and with only Ezra Cain to help me."

"What was that like?" I said, glad to catch my breath.

"Oh, he was a hard worker, Ezra Cain, but he had odd notions. He always said there was a panther here on Wicked Hill."

"A panther!"

Peachie nodded. "Said he heard it at night. It screamed like a woman." The cook laughed. "Here he was on Wicked Hill surrounded by women, and he hears a woman's scream and thinks panther."

I wiped my forehead and asked, "That's the farm hand the sisters run off?"

"The very same, him and the peddler man. They left without their wages."

I frowned. "How could those two run off two working men, anyways?"

Peachie's eyes grew wide. "With switches! Those two men made tracks in a cloud of dust."

"You saw?" I asked.

"I saw the sisters come down from the top of Wicked Hill and chase off the men with sticks in their hands," Peachie said. "That was right after my old Mam had died. Miss Marietta and Miss Henrietta had taken their spinning wheels to the top of Wicked Hill to watch the wind turn the wheels. That was the first queer thing to happen on Wicked Hill, and the next was when those men left in a cloud of dust."

"Hmmph!" I snorted. "I'll not be run off so easily!"

On I worked through the rooms of farmhouse each week, every day fetching more ferns for Miss Marietta, and searching for the star key each night. Sometimes I would be left alone in my dreams with no one to work me. Then I became scared, for there was always something there in the dark, flapping unseen, ready to chase me through my dreams until I heard cockcrow and could waken.

I woke in a dream and worked in a dream until nightfall when I fell asleep to dream some more. The weeks stretched on until I worried I had forgotten what day it was, there without a calendar or a clock, except the cursed clock in the cookhouse.

Then I woke in the middle of night, with Peachie shaking me. "Wake up, wake up," she whispered. "It's midnight. Make haste!"

She got me up and got me dressed and got me out in the starry night that was spitting snow. By the light of the pour lamp we made our way up the path to the cowshed. "Unbar the door, but be quiet," she whispered.

We slipped in and closed the barn door. Once inside she raised the lantern aloft and pointed to Brownie Belle. "Look! Look! They kneel, just as is told."

Then I knew it was Christmas Day. We both stood there watching Brownie Belle kneel well into the morning until a soft pale light come from the east and Brownie Belle rose on her own accord. Peachie kept me company while I milked her.

Though Christmas, I could still feel a heavy weight deep in my apron pocket. There had been a burning question I had meant to ask and now seemed as good a time as any.

"How did Miss Henrietta conjure her sister to take the silver penny?"

"Ah!" said Peachie, "That's where one sister proved stronger than the other. One morning shortly after the old clock broke, Miss Marietta comes down to the dining room, and there on the open window sill is a pretty little nosegay of snowdrops and chickweed."

Peachie shut one eye toward me, making me think.

"The language of the flowers," I cried. "What did the pretty little nosegay mean?"

"Snowdrops for hope, and chickweed for a secret meeting."

"Someone hoped for a lover's tryst!" I said.

"Just who do you think that might be?"

"Abel Pratt?" I asked.

Peachie smiled. "Miss Marietta must have thought so, for she grabbed that pretty little nosegay to see if there were a note attached, and guess what she found tied to the ribbon."

"A love note?"

"The silver penny!"

When we got back to the kitchen, I started to leave the milk pail to cool on the porch, but Mistress Fortune told me to bring it inside. "Have you ever had coco?" she asked, but did not stay for answer. She took out her box of coco and I got the copper saucepan. With well water and brown powder, she made a paste that looked dark and rich. I stuck my finger in to taste.

"Too bitter!" I cried.

Mistress Fortune smiled. "You must take the bitter with the sweet," she said, adding sugar, "and always with a pinch of salt," she added tossing a pinch of salt in the mix. I poured milk from the pail until Peachie said halt.

"Now, stir," ordered the cook, "and I'll show you something." She reached into the white bib she always wore and pulled out a small gold chain. At the end hung a small gold coin. "The Wicks gold," she told me.

"How come the Wicks?" I asked.

"My old Mam gave this to me one Christmas," she said rubbing it with her sleeve. "It belonged to the Wicks."

"Oh!" I answered still not sure what was meant.

Mistress Fortune frowned at me. "It was her way of giving me some of the Wicks gold," she explained.

"Oh!" I said and stirred some more.

Peachie held the coin up to gaze upon it. "We both knew the gold was not for me. My old Mam and I. 'Peachie,' she said, 'life is not fair. You must take the bitter with the sweet.'"

"Wait! What gold?" I asked all confused.

"The Wicks gold! The gold that the Old Gentleman brought back at the end of the war. He came back with bags of gold and Ezra Cain to serve him, just as he had on the battlefield. Nobody thought to look for gold on Wicked Hill, and here it stayed long after the Old Gentleman's death. When the time come for my old Mam to die, she was afeared to leave the gold for her daughters to fight over, so she had Ezra Cain and Abel Pratt build that big treasure house on the windy side of Wicked Hill."

"The Wicks sepulcher?" I said, still not hardly following.

Peachie nodded. "Only one person is buried inside and that's my old Mam. She had the gold buried with her. To one daughter she told half the secret to get the gold and to the other daughter she told the other half. She thought that in time they would learn to work together to find the gold together and then share the gold together." Peachie Fortune laughed. "They studied and practiced and now know many things, but together they have yet to learn that!"

"How did she get the gold in the tomb with nobody's help?"

"She couldn't. She needed me," Peachie said. "I put the gold in the sepulcher like she told me right before she died, before the two started looking for it. When the tomb was sealed, the sisters realized what their old mam had done, and they remembered all what she had been telling them for days on her deathbed, but they feared to confide in one another. Then they began to think on the men who built the sepulcher. They feared them, as if Ezra Cain and Abel Pratt would rob them of their inheritance! One man they both loved, but they ran him off from Wicked Hill in case he might know their secret. They were too afraid to ask me. Men, they could do without, but they cannot do without me." Peachie put the gold chain back under her white bib and turned to me. "Do you like gingerbread?"

CHAPTER XI: LIKE BREAD
LOVES SALT

Witches cannot cross running water.
— 2001 Southern Superstitions

That day was my last good day on Wicked Hill.
Christmas came and went — and a week later — New
Years came and went too. I was in that little back
room filled with books, holding the lamp for Miss Henrietta
poring over her blueprints. "Higher, higher," she'd say,
though my arm was tired.

All of a sudden, I heard gunfire down the river. Seconds
later I heard another gunshot. Then seconds after that, I
heard another gun fire, until all the way up the river folks
knew it was midnight and a new year begun. Meanwhile
Miss Henrietta kept after me to hold the lamp higher, higher
on into the night.

Shortly after New Years Brownie Belle got sick. When I
led her to the knoll outside the cowshed, the poor old thing
buckled at the knees. I had to tug and tug to get her up and
back in her stall. Then I ran to the cookhouse and told the
cook.

"It's the falling sickness!" Mistress Fortune cried.

"Can you cure her?" I begged.

The cook looked grim and shook her head. "We must
tell Miss Henrietta."

"The cow can't die here!" Miss Henrietta cried when told the news. She gestured around her cluttered pantry. "We can't any of us dispose of the body and think of the vermin her carcass would attract."

"But a good milker is like a member of the family!" I wailed.

"What about the milk?" the cook asked her mistress.

"Oh." Miss Henrietta sat back in her rocker and thought. "Better get the book of recipes." She looked around. "Where did it get to?"

I knew where. Miss Marietta had me borrow it back the other day, but I knew better than to say so. I ran from the room, out the backdoor, and down the path to the cabin where Miss Marietta sat fretting in her bed.

"There you come," she cried when I burst through the cabin door. "Where's my Dittany tea?"

She forgot about tea quick enough when she learned of the cow. Grabbing the book of recipes and wrapping a blanket around her thin shoulders, she slipped into her stout shoes and marched up the path to the farmhouse. There she stood flat-footed, unwilling to enter her old home. Her sister had to hoist her heavy weight out of the rocker and stagger into the hallway to ease herself through the backdoor and down the steps of the porch where the wind was spitting snow.

Miss Henrietta had her reaching stick she used as a walking cane to cross the sandy ground of the barnyard. "You brought the book?" she asked.

"What about the cow?" her sister replied. "She can't stay here."

Peachie Fortune turned to me. "You must take the cow down to the fields below the cowshed. But first go to the workshop and bring the mallet."

With the tip of her stick, Miss Henrietta idly drew in the sand.

"Why the mallet?" I asked.

Miss Henrietta answered. "To club the cow and dash her brains out. Then leave her for the wolves."

"Better leave her dead to the wolves than alive," said Miss Marietta.

Her cook nodded sadly. "It would be the kindest thing," she said.

I was dumbstruck. Me? Hit Brownie Belle!

"I found something," Miss Marietta said, looking up from the book.

We all stopped and then stared at that strange little book with the speckled leather binding while Miss Marietta read aloud. "Any good neighbor can borrow milk from another if she has a long enough reach."

As we stood together with our feet pointing inward, Miss Henrietta scratched a line with her reaching stick from one foot to the next until she described a circle in the sand.

"There's more," said Miss Marietta. "Like unto like. Like bread loves salt."

"I brought the salt," said Peachie, holding up a knotted handkerchief.

Miss Henrietta drew another squiggly line in the sand. "We're ready," she said. We stepped back as Mistress Fortune poured salt from her hanky in the grooves made by the reaching stick until the salt made a crescent outline. Miss Henrietta smiled one of her few smiles. "And the cow jumps over the moon."

Meanwhile I must go to the workshop and grab the mallet and take Brownie Belle to her doom. "And don't take all day!" the cook yelled after me as I walked slowly away. Brownie Belle looked glad to see me, even with the mallet in my hand. I led her gently toward the knoll and then down the broad hillside to the fields below the barn. Who knows the last time those fields had been mowed, but the winter had killed off or frozen whatever grew there. We walked the snowy ground without Brownie Belle slipping once. Where the two fields meet is an old split rail fence more than three rails high. There I swung the mallet and left my dear sweet Brownie Belle in one of the fence's zig-zag corners and slowly made my way back up the hill.

The cook inspected the mallet, like I knew she would, and was well satisfied. "It had to be done, Amy Scoggins," Mistress Fortune told me. "What must be is no wickedness." I did not answer and she let me alone.

That evening as I was about to take my leave of Miss Henrietta, I mentioned to her how cold the air had gotten. "Will you be warm enough?" I asked her as she sat there in her old armchair with nothing on but her Mother Hubbard of blue Bedford Cord.

"Better bring me a blanket," she said.

"How about a pretty quilt from the loom room?" I asked. "I don't mind climbing the stairs."

That long woolly brow of hers shot up and her dull eyes took on a shine in the dim light. "I'd forgotten those quilts were there. Bring me the blue one with the broken dishes pattern. My mama made that for me when I was a little girl."

I slipped upstairs into the loom room and hurried past the two spinning wheels to the cedar chest against the wall. I knew the quilt she meant, but I also took the Martha Washington Flower Garden quilt as well. Taking the back steps through the trapdoor in the sleeping porch, I left one quilt in the pantry and brought the other to the room full of books.

As I gave her the quilt, I asked, "Are those spinning wheels balanced right? When I went out of the loom room I could have swore the wheels began to rock."

Miss Henrietta gave out a low chuckle. "Better beware. They say when spinning wheels turn on their own, they've caught a ghost."

I laughed too and tucked Miss Henrietta in for the evening, before slipping out the back way with the stolen quilt in my arms. Down the path to the cookhouse I ran, but at the barn I turned, and I sped down the broad hillside to the fence where two fields meet.

It was turning cold, like I told Miss Henrietta, and I was worried for Brownie Belle, who was not dead. I lied. I passed by the wet stump where earlier I had pounded the tip of the cow's tail until hairs were stuck in the mallet. That's what pleased Mistress Fortune when she asked to see.

In the twilight came a soft lowing telling me the little gal was still alive. I laid the heavy quilt, tent-like, over the corner of the split rail fence. It sheltered Brownie Belle almost like a stall in a cowshed. I rubbed her sides and then turned her head in my hands so I might look into her eyes. "I'll never desert you," I promised. Then I had to leave.

The world of the two white fields was utterly still, but as I walked the distance I heard a far cry, like a squalling baby on the wind. The cries followed me all the way back up the hill and on to the cabin where I next had to see to Miss Marietta for the night. She was in rare form, and had set out a new bottle of wine to pour herself a glass. This wine poured white, not red. When I mentioned that I heard a baby's cry, my lady's eyes would not meet mine.

"You're hearing things," she said turning away. "Where could there be a baby around here?"

I thought a moment. "There's the farmer with the white horse who gave me a ride in his wagon. His wife could have delivered him a son."

Miss Marietta scoffed, "And you think you can hear a baby cry miles away?" Then she batted her pale blue eyes. "Have a drink," she said. "It will calm your nerves."

I shook my head no.

"Tut, tut," she said. "Tis but a potion of wildflowers fermented in honey. Drink!"

I cast my eyes down. "Mistress Fortune would not like it, nor would I blame her."

My lady answered, "Mistress Fortune need not know. You could take your little tin cup off the shelf and drink from that. She'll never suspect."

I hesitated, for my mouth watered, but I still went about my chores. As I plumped her cushion behind her back, I asked Miss Marietta, "What did the book mean when it said, 'like bread loves salt'?"

"Because bread needs salt to have flavor," she said, settling in her cushions. She waved a knobby finger in the air. "Find the essence of a thing and you have the thing itself."

I thought on that as I hurried away, off to the split-rail fence where I slept, leaning against Brownie Belle until early dawn. Outdoors the slightest light can wake one, but what woke me was a baby's cry coming again on the wind over the river. I walked back to the cookhouse with that wailful sound in my ears.

As I passed the open cowshed, I saw the milk can that I had emptied and scalded clean the day before. Wondering why it was there, I picked it up expecting it to be empty, but it was heavy and I could feel something sloshing inside. Running down the path holding tight to the lid, I saw Peachie Fortune already up and standing at the cookhouse door.

"Good! You brought it. Bring it in." Inside she pried loose the lid to the milk can. About a third of the can was filled with milk, which poured thin and blue into the milk jug.

"Where did it come from?" I asked.

"The book of recipes can solve any problem," Mistress Fortune answered. "Here on Wicked Hill and all the wide world beyond is open to the book of recipes."

My forehead wrinkled up in thought. "Like bread loves salt. You know that old story?" I asked.

Peachie nodded. "After the war we had a lot of travelers passing through. They told the story, out of homesickness, I guess."

I was about to say more when we heard footsteps. Both Miss Henrietta and Miss Marietta arrived at the cookhouse from different paths. Each seemed as anxious as the other to see what the book of recipes had wrought.

"There was milk?" asked Miss Marietta.

"But not much of it," said Miss Henrietta peering inside.

Miss Marietta sniffed. "There will be even less tomorrow," she said.

Miss Henrietta looked up at both of us. "Better start saving egg shells."

That struck me as odd, saving egg shells, but no odder than most goings-on on Wicked Hill. I kept quiet and out of the way, which was hard, for the weather was cold, and only a few rooms had fires. My poor hands were red and raw. They never quite got warm enough, except when scalding the milk can, which I was told to leave in the cowshed for the night. There I quickly made my way down the broad hillside for the fence where two fields meet. In the zig-zag corner of the split rail fence, I found the Martha Washingtons Flower Garden quilt, but no cow underneath.

Poor Brownie Belle had staggered off to crop the frozen grass and had fallen near that old wet stump. It took all my breath, pushing and pulling and propping her up, to get that cow back on her feet and standing in her corner under the flowered quilt.

By dark I had her quieted. Just as I started to go, there again I heard over the wind from the river a squalling baby's cry. The cry came faint, but clear. It seemed nowhere close by, as Miss Marietta pointed out, and I could not, for the life of me, understand how I could hear it.

That evening I asked Miss Henrietta what she thought.

"You're crazy! That's what I think," she told me. "People who hear things are soft in the head and not to be trusted. What about that old man in the Bible who heard voices and nearly kilt his own son?"

"Father Abraham!" I cried.

"Sometimes we mistake what we hear," Miss Henrietta went on to say. "There's no mischief in a simple mistake, but those who listen to what clearly is not there are only inviting madness!"

"I keep hearing a baby cry!"

"Because you listen for it," my lady snapped. "Do you know what happens to people who grow mad? They're taken off in a wagon with bars like circus animals and locked up in a big stone house with all the others who rave both night and day. Is that what you want for the rest of your life, girl?"

She must have seen the fear in my eyes as I shook my head no, for she breathed easier. "Good. Then we'll hear no more about it," she said and turned to her dinner of Indian pudding, creamed corn, and bacon burgoo.

That night was bitter cold, worse than the night before, for the sky was no longer clear. Mists from the river rolled over the fields. Brownie Belle and I were wrapped in a fog surrounded by darkness. Nothing to see, only sounds to hear.

There in the crook of the split-rail fence, we were sheltered from the wind, so I could stand the cold, only my feet were damp and I feared the ague. Stamping in place, up and down, to keep my feet warm, I dearly wanted to leave for my own warm pallet in the cookhouse loft, but I could hear strange calls and cries from the woods beyond, and feared just as much as the ague to leave Brownie Belle alone. Finally, stupid and tired, I drifted off to sleep resting my head on my dear friend's warm side, and the last thing I heard was a baby's cry.

Early the next day, before cockcrow, I made my way to the cookhouse glad to get warm. When I passed the cowshed, there was the milk can, shining in the early morning light, and once more there was fresh milk on Wicked Hill, though how or why I could not say.

"It's the book of recipes," Peachie Fortune explained. "You're not an educated girl," she told me. "There are things you don't know, so there is much you don't understand."

"I may be plain spoken," I said, "but that don't mean I'm simple-minded. I'm like the girl in that story."

"What story?" the cook asked impatiently.

"There was this here king," I told her, "who had a daughter that he loved very much. He gave her a gold crown and new dress every birthday, and on her fifteenth birthday he took her on his knee and said, "Honey, tell me how you love me!"

Peachie's old hatchet face broke into a grin, for she knew the story well. "And the girl told her father," she said, "'I love you like bread loves salt.'"

"Only that pert reply displeased the old king," I said, "who expected to a fancier answer."

Peachie nodded, "So he turned his only beloved daughter out of his house."

"And she had to take a poor man to marry her," I added.

"But only if she came to him in her shift," Peachie said.

I nodded. "It was a shift wedding, so he wouldn't have to pay any of her debts."

Peachie leaned back from the egg shells she was separating. "I heered tell, it was a good marriage none-theless."

"Oh, yes," I said. "They were good people who worked hard, and had a farm, and a house full of kids until one day, years later, the girl heard that her father, the king, was poorly."

Peachie shrugged. "What could she do?"

I told her. "She rushed to the old king's side," I said. "She nursed him through the worst of it and the old king was shamed. He asked, 'How could you come back to care for one who treated you so ill,' and she answered, 'Because I love you, like bread loves salt. Without salt, bread has no savor. Oh, how flat and stale this life would be without you in it!'"

Peachie looked up from her egg sorting. "I wonder what that story would be like," she asked, "if the girl had a maw and not a paw."

Since both of us were orphans, neither could say, so I asked instead, "Why do they need eggshells?"

The cook looked sly. "Folks around here break their eggshells. They say witches go to sea in them."

I laughed out loud. Such a notion! That whale of a Miss Henrietta Wicks sitting somehow in an eggshell bust my sides.

Mistress Fortune gave me a cross look. "Laugh all you like, but we are in dire straits. Crossing that river in this weather will be no mean feat. Then walking on foot! And don't expect your friendly farmer with the white horse to give out rides. No one will stop for anyone from Wicked Hill."

When the two sisters came to collect the egg shells, they were displeased with the milk.

"There's less here than the time before," said Miss Marietta.

"That's why we have the eggshells," Miss Henrietta told her.

Miss Marietta turned to Peachie Fortune. "We'll need a fire."

Peachie looked at me. "Back of the cookhouse is the old iron cauldron. Set it to rights, and I'll wipe it down while you fetch two pails from the well-sweep."

As I brought the water, Peachie wiped down the old iron pot and built a fire beneath it. We poured in both buckets while the two sisters sat at the table in the cookhouse sorting their eggshells.

I left the cook as she bent over her fire and slipped off to see Brownie Belle. When I passed through the open cowshed, I stepped into the stillness of the white world, with no whining winds whipping about the ears. I began to breathe easy and even wonder if I had heard what I heard, or if indeed I had heard anything at all. Then I thought back on the past night and I sniggered into my sleeve at how I had acted. Maybe I got cabin fever.

I knew I could be gone all afternoon so long as I come back with an armload of firewood, so I decided to slow my pace. I thought what it would be like to have no duties and none to worry about. Happy to be all alone, I wanted to enjoy the emptiness all around me until I made my way to the crook in the zig-zag fence.

There the quilt still hung, but Brownie Belle was gone! I scanned the snow for any hoof prints of my friend. Then I thought, were there really wolves? Here on Wicked Hill I wouldn't doubt it.

That's when I broke down and cried. I sat on that wet black stump, and I cried and I cried till my eyes went dry. I cried for Brownie Belle. I cried for Paw and Maw. I cried for Davy. Then I shut up.

I set out to search. Up and down both fields I called for Brownie Belle until it started to rain. Big wet snowdrops splashed all around me. I hurried back to the fence and grabbed the Martha Washington Flower Garden quilt for cover. Just before I wrapped it around my head, I heard something else on the wind. No babe this time. This time it was the scream of a woman.

A panther! I thought. A panther screams like a woman. A panther got Brownie Belle, or did the wolves? I wondered. Then I thought, are there any still around about to get me! I set out running up that broad, slippery hillside. At the cowshed I stowed the wet Martha Washington Flower Garden quilt and grabbed firewood from the wood stack nearby.

Outside the cookhouse but sheltered from the cold rain, the three women still confabbed over their fire. The water had warmed enough to send up little vapors of steam in the dim winter air. Peachie Fortune was bending over the water with Miss Marietta sitting on her haunches and Miss Henrietta squatting square on the earth with her legs crossed. All three were carefully setting adrift eggshells upon the dark waters.

Then, in the distance, I heard it again. A woman's scream, no panther! What I heard was sorrow, the sorrow of a woman unconsolable. I cried out at the sound of it.

"Don't tell me you don't hear that!"

Both sisters looked at each other. Their eyes met.

"She sees," Miss Henrietta said.

"I hear things, not see things!" I cried.

"Hush, girl, go up to your loft and keep out of the way," said Peachie Fortune pushing me off.

The others looked up and stared at me until I felt the force of all six eyes. I went inside whimpering as I crawled up the steps to my pallet where the smell of lye choked me. I could do nothing there but think. I could not help but think about Brownie Belle, which made me remember the baby's cries, and made me wonder about the woman's scream.

Meanwhile, a stillness filled the cookhouse. Was anybody there? Cautiously I climbed down the steps and looked outside. Miss Henrietta, Miss Marietta, and Mistress Fortune were gone.

Calling their names I climbed the path to the farmhouse, thinking they may have strayed up there, but the farmhouse was dark, except for the hall lamp which shone out the backdoor left ajar. It shone enough light for me to see Tabitha sitting by the door, glowering, and guarding the entrance.

Then against the night rang out a woman's scream, and suddenly I was afraid. Never before had I been left all alone on Wicked Hill.

I stepped lively crossing the barnyard and down the path to the cabin, the only other place I could imagine they had gone, for there was always a bright fire on the hearth in the cabin. I entered calling, but already sure that no one was there.

No one was. I warmed my face and hands against the hearth, wondering where to go next, the sepulcher or the swinging bridge. Turning around to warm my backside, I faced the sideboard. There next to the bottle of wine set my little tin cup, as if waiting for me. No one would know, I remembered.

The screams of the desperate woman were still ringing in my ears, so I poured me a stiff one. The white wine was thick and sugary like syrup, but tasted like medicine. No sooner did I set the cup down than the noises stopped.

For the rest of the night I floated, feeling neither the cold nor fearing the dark. When I got back to the deserted cookhouse, I barely noticed on the kitchen table the gallon of milk, the pound of butter, and the side of bacon. It is not that I saw unclearly; I saw clearly enough, but at a great distance, far out of earshot of any women, or babies, or cows, nor did I notice as I drifted to sleep that the last sound I heard seemed to be the cry of wolves.

CHAPTER XII: THE WITCH'S MIRROR

When a witch is at her mischief, she is invisible to everybody except the person bewitched.
                    —2001 *Southern Superstitions*

That night I dreamed strange dreams. I dreamt that I drank blood. Warm and salty on my throat, I could taste blood, which is strange to say, for never before had I tasted anything in dreams until then.

In my dream I run down the broad hillside naked as the wind. I leap over the high split-rail fence and seem to fly across the white frost of the farther field and into the woods beyond. Far off I can hear howls. Somewhere wolves gather. I pause to listen, for wolves are my prey.

The night now no longer holds any terrors for me. I can see as well as all the other night critters—coons and beavers, night owls and weasels—I scatter in my wake. In a clearing, I suddenly stop. My feet land, and I am on all fours.

There in twilight is another just like me, a solid black panther shining like velvet. We square off, and my sister screams like a woman, and I scream back at her, just like a woman who has had enough!

My sister bares her teeth at me, then looks away and leaps off, expecting me to follow. We lope through the dark toward the shoals of that all-devouring river. At the bend on a rocky reef, a rangy pack of wolves tear at some dead thing. Some poor thing had wandered off the fields to die at the bend of that all-devouring river. Nothing is left to know what once the poor thing was, only a rag of skin, a broken bone, and hank of hair.

Screaming like a woman who screams for vengeance, I pounce. Weak and underfed, those four young wolves are no match for the two of us, as we turn and toss them in the air, snapping bones with our jaws. My sister worries the first by the neck till I hear it snap, and then she throats the second with her shiny teeth. I hold down my wolf with one paw and rip down its side with the other. That's when I drink blood, salty and warm down my neck and throat. The fourth one gets away. With a yelp it limps off into the river and swims for the other side.

No thought of anything but the chase, I leap into those dark, riling waters to swim after him. Well into the middle of that raging river we meet. We fight and I leave him there for the all-devouring river to bear away.

Up I rush to the opposite bank, feeling the wet red clay squish between my toes. I lope along a wire fence where a white horse whinnies in alarm. Sliding under the wire, I chase the white horse across the unplowed farmland toward a little light in the distance, but lose him by an open hole recently dug in that frozen ground and in this weather. I nose about the open hole, curious-like, feeling the wet red clay between my toes, then lope off to inspect the light coming over the rise.

The light shines in one room of the dark farmhouse where a circle of silent people sit utterly still around a long table. Seeing their sad eyes and bowed heads, I lose all scent of the chase, all thrill of the hunt. One of them I seem to know, but cannot remember how. He stares at the woman across from him who stares at a little bundle on the table, silent and still. I scream once more like a woman screams when there is naught else to do but scream at the blackness all around her.

A panther no longer, I stand once more upright. I am in my altogether. My two bare feet planted in the wet red clay, I scream up into the night once more for the sheer thrill of screaming, with a cry to shatter all the stars.

Such a dream! So real it seemed! When I woke first thing in the morning, I could still feel a raw wetness between my toes. I flung back my covers to check my feet, half expecting to find the red clay from my dream. Would you know what I found there? Not red clay. Red blood!

CHAPTER XIII: THE WITCH'S SEAT

One who teaches witchcraft to more than three people will herself lose the power.

—2001 *Southern Superstitions*

Once Brownie Belle was gone, winter settled on Wicked Hill. Then came the blue snow and the black ice with the dark skies and the ever moaning wind and shuddering ground on Wicked Hill. On I worked without stopping, for the chores could not quite get done. The laundry never quite got dry. We wore it damp and all caught the sniffles, and I was blamed for that! The last time I took the hot water to scald the outhouse, a thin coat of ice formed on the seat, and I heard about that from Miss Henrietta, and Miss Marietta, and even Mistress Fortune, who scolded me the worst! My days were spent rising in the dark and working in the dim light through the long day on into the night. After Brownie Belle's death, I resolved not to be a prey to dreams, even if it meant not sleeping, so I would spend many a black night staring out into the darkness until the first sign of dawn, only to catch twenty winks before cockcrow.

Though bone tired and weary, I worked like a fury. Too hard I worked, and it showed. I rubbed holes in sheets washing them. I broke dishes drying them.

Chairs would scatter when I entered a room. Finally Peachie Fortune sat me down.

"What ails you?" she asked. "You look hag-ridden."

I thought of the many nights I had walked with one sister or the other looking for the star key.

"Do you have a fever?" she asked. She put her hand to my forehead. "A little warm, perhaps. Better burn it out." She looked out the window at the sleet. "Take the ladder and go wash the windows in the barn."

I grabbed my shawl on the coat hook and trudged on to my work. That pretty barn had windows down below and up above. Every wall had windows and none seemed to have been cleaned since the men folk had been run off Wicked Hill a long time ago. The weather was still cold, but the wind was quiet, as I set out with rag and bucket to wash the twenty windows of the old horse barn. Washing the outside panes was cold work but cheerful in the outdoors. The sleet that fell upon my forehead felt cool to the touch. Before my eyes were little stars of light.

Washing the inside panes was less drafty but dreary in the half dark. The workshop had windows all around, so Abel Pratt could carve his stone. He had to leave his work behind when he was run off Wicked Hill. There was a half angel with one wing, a clump of lilies set in stone, and a stone slab with a little lamb on top. They lay around the work table. I fingered the many tools left lying about, the hammers and saws, the drill and drill bits, and thought of Paw and what he would have done with these tools. How could any man leave such precious means to earn a living? They must have scared him good, or else he was too shamed and disheartened to take away what was his.

There were no windows in the tack room where Ezra Cain stayed year in and year out. I wondered what kind of man would hole up in the barn waiting only for the day he would be turned away. Abel Pratt seemed a better sort somehow, at least more important, but he had no room at all on Wicked Hill. Peachie told me how he stayed up in the barn loft with hay for his pillow. I looked up at the dwindling light. At least he had windows aloft.

I climbed up the ladder to clean the windows which pulled in so I could get both sides. While rubbing away in the winter light, I saw through the glass pane into the hayloft where something shiny brightened one of the corners. I brushed some cobwebs aside and found my first mirror on Wicked Hill.

Perhaps the bit of glass belonged to Abel Pratt who must have used it to part his curly brown hair. Broken and dirty it still stood up on a crossbeam for me to see myself, but that plump, pretty girl was no more. My crowning glory was no longer curly, but wild and dry like the mugwort that grew on the windy side of Wicked Hill. My eyes, once so bright and merry, were sunken into two dark sockets, and my mouth held a brown sullen frown. Maybe because my lips were chapped and broken with an ugly sore. I turned the little cracked mirror's face to the wall, so I did not have to see myself. Now I knew why the Wicks allowed no mirrors on their walls. The thought occurred to me that the more I understood them, the more like them I became. The rest of the work went slowly through the long afternoon.

When I got back to the cookhouse, it was dark. "What took you so long?" Peachie asked. "Come here, let's feel your forehead."

I bent my head to receive her cool touch.

"I hope you aren't coming down with a fever," she scolded.

"I left Fool's Gap to get away from a fever," I said. "I'd hate to think for all my trouble I would get one here."

Peachie stopped fretting and looked me in the eye. "What caused you to come here in the first place?" she asked.

"I was sent here by Miss Juanita Jenkins. She wrote a letter to get me this job."

The old hatchet face frowned. "But how did your Miss Juanita Jenkins know there was a job here? How did she know about Wicked Hill?"

I thought for a moment. The question never came to me before.

I reasoned it out aloud. "Before she died, she called me into her sickroom and gave me a letter. Amy, she said, when I go, I want you to go here—and the envelope was marked Wicked Hill."

Peachie Fortune shook her head. "I still don't understand. It don't make sense. What kind of woman was she, your Miss Jenkins?"

"Oh, a fine 'un," I assured her. "She always was dressed up to the nines and wore powder and rouge and little yellow gloves."

Peachie looked up and caught me with her eye. "She was a church-going woman, you said?"

"Oh, yes," I assured her. "Why Miss Juanita Jenkins was there whenever they let the doors open."

Peachie looked suspicious. "Where did she sit during Sunday service?"

"She was the choir leader," I explained. "She stood before the choir or else she sat at the pianee to play the hymns."

"Did she face the preacher when he read the text?" Peachie Fortune asked.

I thought for a moment, remembering. "No'm," I said. "She always sat ramrod straight on the pianee bench facing the wall."

"She was a witch!" Peachie declared.

"She was a lady!" I cried. "Too much of a lady to crane her neck. A lady never looks back, she would say."

"A witch never faces the preacher when he preaches," Peachie countered. "That's how you can always tell a witch in church."

I shook my head wearily. There was much this cook did not understand. "But Miss Juanita Jenkins was one of the mainstays of our little church in Fool's Gap."

"She was a witch," Peachie declared. "That's how she knew about the job here. They stay in touch with one another by secret means."

"Miss Juanita Jenkins lived her whole life in Fool's Gap, beloved by all. In her life she took on three different orphan girls and raised them proper and sent them out into the world."

"Never to be heard of again, I reckon," said Peachie peevishly.

"Two were before my time, so I don't know, but then there's me," I added a little worried.

"A witch can teach her magic to only three and then must die," Peachie said. "How did you come to stay with her?" she asked.

"My paw caught the fever, and died of it, and my maw caught the palsy after nursing him, and died of it, so Miss Juanita Jenkins had me stay with her. She trained me to be a hired girl."

For a split second then, I was no longer on Wicked Hill. I was back at Fool's Gaps waving good-bye to little Davy Snodgrass as I went to live with Miss Juanita Jenkins. As long as I knew her, she had a little hard bump at her breast. She always had me feel for it when I undressed her for bed. In time, more bumps came and Miss Juanita told me that she was going to die. Instead of taking to her bed, she spent her last days in good works. As the fever spread through the valley, she and I would bring the sick a certain sweet soup she made called negus. Everyone in Fool's Gap raved about Miss Juanita Jenkins' negus soup. Whenever anybody asked for the recipe, Miss Juanita would look sly and claim it had secret ingredients that only she and her girls knew. She showed me once the bottle that held the secret, only I could not spell the word.

"Amy Scoggins, are you in a trance? Speak to me!" Peachie Fortune cried.

I sighed. "For a woman firm in good works I never saw that the soup ever helped."

"What soup?" asked the cook, naturally interested.

"The negus, a thin white soup that's sweet to the tongue," I said. "It was her specialty. For many a bowl I have seen her pour out, and yet I can't think of any that touched her lips."

Peachie Fortune snorted. "Cooks never eat their own poison."

Suddenly I was back in Miss Juanita's kitchen. Taste this, Amy, she'd say, do I need more salt, do I need more mace, but I never knew her to taste the soup herself.

"There was a secret ingredient," I told Peachie. "Miss Jenkins kept it in a bottle with a label I could not spell. The letters were all twisty. But I could make out some. P something, something, S, something, N." I looked at Peachie and Peachie looked at me, and I knew what that word spelt.

That's when Peachie Fortune grabbed me and clasped me in her boney arms. I kicked and pulled like a hare in a trap, but Peachie just held me tight, whispering in my ear, "You got grit, Amy Scoggins, you got grit," until finally worn out with wrestling her, I closed my eyes and fell asleep for the first time in weeks.

CHAPTER XIV: THE WITCH'S SIEVE

If you hang a bread sifter on a door knob at night, you will find witches in it the next morning.
                                    —2001 *Southern Superstitions*

I woke to the sound of bells. Church bells? I wondered. I opened my eyes to sunlight sifting through silver mesh. What was I sleeping under? I pulled off the stiff tin cone and sat up wondering how the flour sieve got there.

"You awake?" called Peachie. In a trice that old hatchet face peered up the steps of the loft and smiled in on me. "I let you sleep in this morning. You needed it. Did you dream last night?"

I rubbed my hair and yawned. "First night since I can remember, no."

Peachie grinned nodding her head up and down. "I knew how it would be, if I used the flour sieve."

"Why did you put that old thing on me?" I asked, a little cross at the notion.

"So as you'd sleep well!" she claimed.

Just then I heard the bell. It was the dinner bell. There was another moot called on Wicked Hill. We hurried up the path to the henhouse where Miss Henrietta and Miss Marietta waited.

Miss Henrietta held a dead Blue Holland by its broken neck. "Lookee here," she cried. "Look what something done!"

"Is it possum or a coon, sister?" asked Miss Marietta.

"Or a polecat?" suggested Peachie.

"Where were you last night?" asked Miss Henrietta staring straight at me.

"I was here," I said. "Where would I be?"

"I missed you last night," said Miss Henrietta.

"So did I," said Miss Marietta. Both sisters looked at me suspiciously.

"You don't think the child killed your precious chicken!" argued Peachie Fortune.

"Can you vouch for her, Mistress Fortune?"

"I can, but I need not!" replied Peachie.

I stopped their fussing. "I know what killed that yard bird," I said.

The three old women stood and stared.

"CAW!" I cried, and out the top of a big cedar tree, a red-tailed hawk flew off into the woods.

"A chicken hawk!" cried Miss Marietta.

"Tabitha!" called Miss Henrietta. Out from under the back porch, the black cat shot into the woods as well.

"Give the bird to me," said Peachie Fortune, " and I'll fix chicken and dumplings for supper."

As we headed back to the cookhouse, I asked, "Has that cat gone after the hawk?"

"Worse," said Peachie. "It was born in May. May cats are always bad for catching snakes and bringing them indoors. That's what Miss Henrietta wants though."

"A snake!"

"A snake's skin. That'll scare off the hawk, if nailed to the roof of the henhouse."

"I'm surprised if it can find a snake this time of year," I said.

"This is the best time to catch a rattler, if that's what you want," said Peachie. "Those snakes are still sluggish in their winter's rest. A babe could pick one up safely and sling it about."

She opened the cookhouse door. Inside she handed me a box of Diamond Head matches. "Light me a stove fire," she told me.

I struck a match. Its blue flame shot up and vanished in the air.

Peachie frowned. "Try again," she said.

I struck another match. This one popped with a puff of smoke, but did not light.

"Once more," said Peachie Fortune and held her breath waiting.

I struck the third match, but it did not catch fire at first. I tried again, but it would not catch. How oddly important it seemed to Peachie whether or not I could strike a match. I was afraid she might never draw breath until I struck fire, so I kept at it with that third match until finally, at last, with a hiss, it burst into a full, warm flame. Peachie let her breath out slow and calm.

I lit the stove and turned to Peachie. "What do I do with the match?" I asked.

"Blow it out," she said and set about her tasks.

To make chicken and dumplings, first the chicken's feathers had to be plucked. The best way was to drop the bird in boiling water, for then the feathers fall right off. I helped her get the big copper pot for the chicken and the smaller copper pot for the dumplings.

As we filled the pots, I asked her, "What did those two sisters mean about missing me last night?"

"The sieve worked," she said.

The truth hit me. "They couldn't get at me," I said. "No dreams."

"Witches can't find their way in and out of the silver mesh of a flour sieve before cockcrow," she said.

"So the hex is broke? I'm free of their spells!"

Peachie took me by the arm and sat me down by the hearth. "You'll not be free as long as you stay on Wicked Hill."

"But last night...."

"Was but one night," Peachie said. "Their hold on you has weakened. It took that third match to light, but light it did. Their magic has turned against them; that chicken died, that's what worried them so. Their will is not to be balked on Wicked Hill, and yet it has." She handed me the box of matches. "Here, put these in your apron pocket. Test yourself. If you can light a fire with the first strike, the spells are broken. If you fail to light three matches in a row, their power over you has returned."

I looked into that sad old hatchet face. "What am I to do?"

"Find the secret heart of their power over you and take it from them."

In the pocket where I put the matches I felt the silver penny. "Or else return the bad luck to them."

Peachie stood and looked out the window. "This morning I saw the fingernail moon."

"That's the third moon since Christmas," I counted.

"Soon the spring thaws," said Peachie. She turned to me. "Promise me to say good-bye before you go."

The rest of the morning and afternoon I took as holiday, my first holiday on Wicked Hill. I roamed the windy side of Wicked Hill above to the lopsided sepulcher of the Wicks, where the fortune of gold was hid, and then to swinging bridge which led me here. This was the side of Wicked Hill that hugged the all-devouring river, running its headless way down the mountainside into the valley below. Snows were melting somewheres. The waters were rising under the footbridge. I could see now why Doris Sawyer left before the spring thaws. Once they came, it would be days before those riling waters would be safe to cross.

I stared long and hard at that swinging bridge and the hard dirt country road on the other side. It would be so easy just to leave now while I could. Peachie would forgive me. Soon another hired girl would come to take my place. As I watched the waters rush away, I felt inside my apron pocket. My hand of its own accord reached for the silver penny beneath the box of matches. Gripping that cursed coin, I knew I would never leave so long as I had it in my grasp. Sadly I turned to climb Wicked Hill once more.

On my way up the steep and rocky road to the farmhouse, I decided what must be done. It would not be simple. It would not be easy. But it must be done today.

The front door to the farmhouse is always locked. I went in the back way and found Miss Henrietta in the pantry skinning a snake on her lap. Tabitha was sunning in the window sill.

"You're here a mite early," she said looking up. "I'll soon have a pretty streamer you can nail above the henhouse door."

"The wash is finally dry," I said. "You want me to change your sheets? It's been awhile."

"Suppose it has," Miss Henrietta said getting up. "I'll help you." By which she meant, she would watch me while I was in her bedroom. I could wander through the whole house except for her bedroom and the room full of books.

The big double bed was a mess, as I knew it would be. Bed covers were twisted in knots and pillows had fallen to the floor. The sheet were gray with little black hairs sticking out. If only I knew the way of the hoodoo, those hairs might mean something other than their general nastiness.

Miss Henrietta stood next to the mantel with the busted clock, her arms crossed as I pulled out all her nasty bedding. As I jerked at the sheets, I noticed the cigar box back on the dresser. I smiled. "I'll take these back to the cookhouse and bring fresh sheets and towels."

"By then the snake skin will be ready."

"Can't wait," I said and sauntered out the door.

No sooner did that backdoor slap shut than I set out lickety-split down the path to the cookhouse where I dumped the dirty sheets out of sight and picked up a clean load of sheets and towels. Then I crossed through the graveyard of hired girls to take the shortcut to the cabin. When I got there, I left the sheets by the door and then knocked. Miss Marietta was at her fire screen still stitching away.

"Fresh laundry," she said without looking up. "Is it that time already?"

"Yes'm. I brung you the first towels that got dry."

"How sweet of you, my dear," she said back to her stitching.

"I was hoping I could ask something of you."

"Anything, my love."

I pulled my hand out of my pocket. "Please take back the silver penny," I begged.

Miss Marietta turned and smiled. "Oh, no, that was for you. For all you do for me. I could not take it back."

"Please take it back. I cannot hide it," I told her. "I cannot lose it," I said. "I cannot be rid of it unless I give it away."

Miss Marietta rose from her stool and faced me. "At last you show some sense. Give it away! But don't be fool enough to let on. Half the fun is the trick itself. There's power in a trick, and the heart of the trick is the surprise. Why not give it to my sister, eh? She'll not be expecting it."

"That's what you want all along, ain't it?" I said. "Something tells me that if I give it to anyone other than you, I'll be bound to you tighter than I already am, like a catspaw to an old cat!"

Miss Marietta chuckled. "You're learning. Good! I can use a bright girl more than a foolish one," she said.

"Perhaps some day we could even be friends," I said, reaching slowly in my pocket.

"Aren't we already, my child?"

"Like mother and daughter," I said.

"Or a favorite teacher and her prize student," she said, and laughed again.

"Yes, ma'am," I said, slipping my hand under the washcloth atop the pile of towels. "Here's your laundry." I pushed my load into her arms, and she quickly let the stack of towels fall to the floor. We both stared as the silver penny popped out.

Suddenly all the smiles disappeared. Her face screwed up dark and gray as the back of her boney hand swung around and hit my face like a thunderclap. "Cheat!" she cried. "Cheat! A cheat is a liar and a liar is a thief! I'll not have any work for me."

I backed toward the door, rubbing my burning cheek. "Just try getting rid of me," I said. "Can you do worse than you've done already? Working me by day and haunting me by night! I'm on to you, and now it is me you must watch, day and night."

Miss Marietta started shouting, but I turned and showed her the back of my head as I sauntered out the front door.

No sooner did that cabin door slam than I ran lickety-split up the path to the farmhouse with the load of sheets in my grasp. Miss Henrietta was there waiting with her snakeskin.

"Took you long enough."

"Your bed will be made by nightfall," I said. I began to pick up pillows to put in the pillows cases. I went about my work slowly with an ear cocked for what I hoped soon would come. And it did!

Out back the dinner bell rang. Someone was pulling on it like a fury.

"Another moot?" Miss Henrietta said. "Twice in day. Is another of my Blue Hollands kilt!" Without giving me another thought she hurried from the room.

I went to the cigar box on the dresser and opened the lid. Inside were little love knots of hair carefully folded and twisted with red thread: three skeins wrapped three times around the silken locks. The silver hair definitely belonged to Miss Marietta, and there was a dark brown curl that must have belonged to Abel Pratt, and white wisps no doubt of the old Mam, but none of my strawberry curls, as Davy Snodgrass calls them.

I heard the backdoor slam. Now Miss Henrietta was bawling at Miss Marietta. I had only seconds, but where could the witch ball be? I remember Mistress Fortune saying to find the heart of their power, just as Miss Marietta said that power is in the heart of the trick. Where did Miss Henrietta put her secret heart? I looked up at the busted clock on the mantel with its glass casement. There was a pink heart painted on the green door.

Outside I could hear Peachie Fortune shouting them both down.

I rushed to the clock. Its little glass door was locked, but I knew from my dreams where to find the key. It stayed in the hidden desk drawer in the back room full of books, and moments later I was able to open the clock's casement door. Inside I found a damp round wad of red hair—my hair! The witch ball. I grabbed it and shut the clock's little glass door, only my guilty conscience made me feel like somebody was watching me. I shivered the way you always shiver when you feel someone is watching you unawares.

"Amy Scoggins!" Miss Marietta cried, and I jumped.

I turned around and met Tabitha glowering at me from the door.

"You answer, girl!" bawled Miss Henrietta.

Tabitha's mouth turned up in what might be a grin if it weren't so sour looking. There I was, alone in her mistress's private room with the forbidden key stealing her secret property. That cat had me to rights and we both knew it. I took a step to the window, but the black cat jumped in my way. She put out one paw and flexed it to show her long silver claws. She hunched her shoulders as if getting ready to spring.

"Annamay Scoggins!" called Peachie Fortune.

I yelled out the open window. "I can't get out," I cried. "The cat won't let me get to the door."

"Tabitha!" bellowed Miss Henrietta.

The black cat yowled as if it had been struck. Then hissing at me, it jumped out the bedroom window, and I ran from the room.

The three old women were waiting for me out by the dinner bell. Their moot could not begin unless we were all there. Peachie was trying to hush Miss Marietta in order to get a straight story out of her while Miss Henrietta was untying her bag of snuff.

Miss Marietta roused herself when she saw me coming and shook a gnarled finger my way.

"That one! That miserable sneak thief."

"What did she steal, sister?" Miss Henrietta asked.

"My peace of mind, my power!" she sputtered.

Peachie rolled her eyes heavenward. "What did the girl do, Marietta?"

"That sly minx tried to palm me the silver penny!"

Miss Henrietta set about roaring with laughter, deep chuckles rumbling in her giant belly.

Peachie Fortune looked at me and frowned. "Do you realize how dangerous it is to play at their own game? Do you wish to be one of them?"

"Here, what's this?" said Miss Henrietta, suddenly sober.

Miss Marietta nodded. "She knows too much."

Miss Henrietta's eyes met hers.

Mistress Fortune turned to me and hissed, "Don't give them ideas."

"I'm not worried," I said in their hearing. "Let them lay in wait for me. They don't dare get rid of me yet. We three are all too close to the gold. I am as close to the gold as they have ever gotten. They depend on me now to work their wills. They cannot afford to let anything happen to me just yet." With that I showed all three of them my back as I sauntered down the path to the cookhouse.

CHAPTER XV:
THE ALL-DEVOURING RIVER

*Life-Demanding Rivers: Just as the sea was held to demand
its toll of human lives, so certain rivers were believed to
require a definite number of lives every year, and to take
them without fail.*

—Christina Hole

I reckon they must have figured that I had gone back to
fetch and carry for them, but I was done with that for
good. Only the Wicks Gold would stop all the mischief
on Wicked Hill. That was the secret heart of its power, for
it was the cause of the mischief in the first place. Next to
the gold the silver penny would seem no more than a dime
next to tens and twenties. They may need me to find the star
key, but I did not need them. I knew how to get to the star
key and how to open that secret treasure room in the Wicks
sepulcher. I knew as soon as I woke up.

I went down the path to the barn. On the table in the
workshop was the star key, as I knew it would be. In plain
sight it rested in the dust with several others just like it.
Only it weren't a key, but a drill bit. When Paw was hale
and hearty, he had quite a toolbox and he showed me all
his tools many a time. The spanners and spoons and plug &
feathers along with the star bit used for cutting stone. I put
one of the star bits into my apron pocket and grabbed the
brace nearby.

My mind was completely clear for the first time in months. All was quiet in the barnyard. The moot was over. Everyone was gone. I climbed the windy side of Wicked Hill with the wind moaning and the ground shuddering under my feet. I was all alone when I reached the sepulcher and found the mossy star in back. Standing among the dead ferns at my feet, I set the star bit into the carving and put the brace to the bit.

I pressed on the brace. It stood as hard as a rock, as if it weren't no more than a piece of the stone tomb itself. I leaned down. Nothing. I rocked back and forth. Nothing. I pushed and pulled and worked up a sweat. Nothing!

Stopping to wipe my brow with my apron's skirt, I saw the ferns at my feet and plucked one for luck. I rubbed it across the carven star and then set the star bit and brace to begin again. This time I no more as leaned on the brace, than to feel it turn beneath me. Out came a deep, muffled groan as the wall to the tomb swept inward like one of the windows in the barn. It moved so quickly I had to stop myself short to keep from falling in.

There was nothing but darkness inside the tomb. I felt behind the door and found a double bar with a hinge in the middle. That double bar would wedge against both sides of the stone door until the hinge was unlatched by the star key.

The late afternoon sun began to make its way into the shadows, or else my eyes grew accustomed to the gloom. I was glad I had stopped when I did, for there was a wide hole just inside the wall where the ground had given way underneath. It was a six-foot drop.

As I looked down, I saw the pale beams of sunlight hit something shiny that glittered up from the depths. I peered into the bottom of the hole and there it was. The Wicks gold. Coins spilt from bags rotted by the damp. They glittered along the sides of the cave-in and led to more treasure below. I tottered at the brink, weighing what to do. For as much as I wanted the gold, the way down was dark, and dangerous, and deep.

Still, there was nothing for it, but to do it, so I held my breath and jumped down the hole onto a little ledge. The ledge was no more than the heap of earth that had given way up above, but it broke my fall so I could slide into the underground gully beneath. Once I landed on the wet rocks below, I cocked my ear ready to jump back up if I heard any noise at all. The only sound I heard was that all-devouring river eating its way through Wicked Hill.

A little further down from where I crouched, stretched a finger of water that must have come from that river with no name. I could see the mound of gold rising like a stream of light up out of the water. I dropped down to touch it. It felt wet and cold sifting through my hands, and that's when I found Dory.

Little Dory with the pretty yellow hair. Her hair was still bright and golden floating on the water, but all the rest of her was gone to corruption: Her bones turned to chalk among the rocks they rested among, her apron and smock sunk into the mud. The sight of her there did not scare me— I had seen death before—it only made me sad.

Poor Dory. She had wanted the gold to make her dreams come true. She too had figured out the secret of the star key and made her way down here, but she had come too late. The spring thaws must have flooded here all of a sudden and trapped her with her treasure. All around her were half empty bags of loot. The rest the all-devouring river bears away.

Then to my ear it seemed to me that the sound of river grew louder as a little wave lapped the toe of my clog. The spring thaws had returned. I had seen the river rise this morning. Here I was no better off than Dory!

I gathered up three bags of gold, enough to carry, and made my way back up the side where the floor of the sepulcher caved in. The light from the late afternoon sun was getting dimmer. Too dim and too sudden, I thought. I looked up to see what's the matter, just in time to find the stone door slowly swinging shut.

Jumping out of my skin I sprang to the slide from the cave-in, my clogs slipping on the wet earth. I spilt one of the bags of gold in my haste. Some coins I caught in my apron pockets as I scrambled up the cave's rocky side. When I reached that little ledge where I had climbed down before, I began to scurry up the wall of the stone sepulcher before the stone door shut for good.

As I hauled myself up, one of the rotten bags ripped and gold fell into the darkness below. Down there sounds were growing louder, as if some great force were rushing in.

I kept on clawing my way up the stone wall as the door glided past me over head. Reaching out, my fingers just grazed where the secret door fit into the wall shutting out the light.

Now deep was the dark that surrounded me. Pitch dark. Never had I known such darkness, for it was truly the darkness of the grave. I held onto the stone wall that closed me in. I dared not step back because of the hole behind me. All the while as I clung to that wet stone wall, down below the rushing sound grew into a roar.

I cannot say how long I stayed there in the dark. My mind left me. It went to countless things, my feeding the sick Miss Juanita's soup, my letting Brownie Belle die, my hearing the baby's cries, and maybe somehow the baby's cries were my fault too. Maybe what's happened to me now was a judgment! Maybe I was one of the wicked now, here on Wicked Hill.

No! What must be is no wickedness. I could not keep poor Brownie Belle from the wolves, nor had I harmed knowingly any babe, or woman, or soup-loving member of the Fool's Gap congregation. Had I not drunk the same sweet negus as all the others? Wake up, Amy Scoggins, and collect your thoughts.

I closed my eyes to find a friendlier darkness than the black surrounding me. I held on tight and just listened until I could hear church bells there in the back of my mind. Then I remembered the matches.

Still inside my apron were the matches Peachie had given me earlier in the day. I filched one and struck it with my thumbnail. No soap. I tried the match a couple of times, but the air seemed too damp. So I tried another, with no luck. I sought a third match. The thought struck me that I might still be under some spell and that I was doomed to darkness if I did not strike fire on the very next try. All my hope and confidence depended on this one match, a new one, that I filched from my pocket. With a little quiet prayer, and a deep breath, I struck the match head.

It burst into light!

Now I could see into all the corners of the sepulcher's secret treasure room. There was the hinge on the bar wedging the wall tight. Hanging down over the hinge was a hook on a line. I fit the hook to the hinge with one hand and pulled while holding the burning match in the other. The hook did not budge, but I did not dare use more force for fear of falling into the rushing water below.

Just as the match was dying out, I looked up and saw a three-legged spindle. Quickly I scanned the stone ceiling. Above me, reaching to the spindle was an arm that connected to a flywheel, and hanging from the flywheel was a pendulum, and a long chain hung with weights. The escapement!

Dropping the burning match, I jumped to the chain, smashing the last bag of gold on the wall. A price well paid, for tugging on the pendulum pulled the chain that turned the flywheel, that turned the arm, that turned the spindle, which pulled the line to unhook the lock on the hinge to unlatch the door.

From the inner wall of the sepulcher I swung one leg over the darkness and nudged with my toe the opposite wall. It swayed on the balanced pivot, and in came a sliver of late afternoon sun.

Carefully I edged along the rim of the sump hole that was filling with water and worked my way back to the light.

Putting both hands on the stone wall and gripping the sides, I pushed with my knee. The wall turned on the pivot and I was swung outside into the fresh air. I was back among the living once more.

I sighed a deep, heavy sigh. Somewhere inside of me all the air went out, all the stale air I had breathed from that wet grave. I held onto the door for a moment breathing in the good clean air and feeling the good warm sun on the back of my neck. I breathed another deep, contented sigh.

Only this time I got shivers, the shivers you get when you think someone's spying on you unawares. Even though you cannot see or hear anything, still you know something is there.

I opened my eyes and turned around, there to see Tabitha crouching in the crepe myrtle, glowering, and ready to pounce.

CHAPTER XVI: THE MAY CAT

Kittens born in May were formerly considered unlucky, and were often drowned for no better reason than the date of their birth. It was also said that they would bring snakes into the house when they were older.

–Christina Holes

Staring at me with those mean yellow eyes, Tabitha made a low growl deep in her gut. That black cat had been the curse of my life here on Wicked Hill. She never liked me to begin with. I was no more to her than some toy to chew on. She led me to the graveyard of the hired girls just out of spite and drew blood to boot when she scratched my cheek. She saw me take the witch ball from Miss Henrietta's broken clock and now was ready to fight me then and there. Always spying, always prying, and somehow always telling on those she caught, Tabitha was always out to get me, get me good.

The black cat arched her back still fixing me with her yellow eyes. There was nowhere to turn, no place to hide. My back was against the wall that could swing open at any moment and cast me into the darkness of the pit. Meanwhile Tabitha inched closer and closer as the growls became louder and louder. Watching her now, I remembered the day we found the moonwort, how she had jumped on my face and climbed up my head to claw my hair. I thought of her creeping into a snake's den and lightly snatching away a fierce rattler for her mistress to gut and skin. How could I hope to win a fight with a devil like that?

I gripped both of sides of the stone wall for support in case the fury of the attack would knock me over. The wall gently moved on the pivot and I nearly fell back into the tomb. I steadied myself and faced my bully, and in that instant Tabitha decided to strike, shrieking as she flew through the air.

Reverend Davy Snodgrass once preached a sermon on bullies, how you got to look them in the eye and face them down, and if you do they won't be bullies no more. Somehow the healing power of God works wordlessly upon the godless through the pious Christian looks of a true believer. I never put much store in that sermon. Bullies are bullies because they can be, I reckon, and Christian looks are like apple pie to those that like to hurt. I will say this, though, for Preacher Davy's message— it's best to look a bully in the eye, for no other reason than you can watch what they're up to. Once Tabitha struck, I was ready for her.

No sooner did I see her spring into action than I pushed with my left shoulder. The stone wall turned on the pivot and became a door swinging backwards as I held on for dear life. Flummoxed, the cat tried stopping in mid-air, but it was too late. Tabitha sailed into the darkness beyond as I pushed with my right shoulder and the stone wall swung shut. No doubt that cursed cat landed on her feet, but she would not like all the water that waited for her below.

It took me a moment to catch my breath. Tabitha was gone to trouble me no more. I think I laughed then, a happy laugh, for the first time on Wicked Hill. I pressed against the stone wall to make sure the hinge was latched and the cat could not find a way out from the way she got in. Sure enough, the stone wall was once again as still as a grave.

The next thing I thought of was Peachie. I had to tell her about Tabitha. I felt my pockets. I had the gold to show her. I remembered Dory. I would have to tell her about Dory too.

I ran back over the windy side of Wicked Hill and through the birch field on my way to the cookhouse. Over the rise I saw the thin line of blue smoke and remembered that Peachie had promised chicken and dumplings for dinner.

However, when I got to the cookhouse, I could tell something was wrong. Gray smoke was coming out the open Dutch door. Black smoke was coming out of the wood stove. I quickly took a pot holder and a dish towel from the pot rack to open the cast iron oven door and removed the chicken that was now burnt dry. Where was Peachie?

Behind me I heard a sound that I could not quite place. When we were young, Little Davy Snodgrass and I would shake dry peas in an empty gourd. That's what this sound was like. I turned, half expecting to see Peachie there behind me. Somehow she had forgot to tend to her cooking. How good it would be to scold Mistress Fortune for a change!

I turned to tell all my news, only to learn more news myself. Instead of the sure tread of Mistress Fortune, there coming down the steps of the loft on its belly was a rattlesnake ready to strike.

Snakes are nothing new to me. Living in the woods I learned to be careful, but still a body can't help but run into snakes every now and then. I knew as long as this old fellow was traveling, he would not strike, but his rattles told me that he wasn't going away. Only when he raised his head and bared his fangs would I be a goner then. There were still the time and the distance to stop him if I moved now.

I looked around for a weapon and grabbed the turning fork from the pot rack. It had a long wooden handle that ended in two barbed tines like a pitchfork. The puncheon floor of the cookhouse stretched a grown man's distance between me the snake. I lunged forward and rammed the fork in the puncheon floor of the cookhouse, catching the rattler's head beneath the fork. The fork stayed wobbling there, stuck between the wooden planks of the floor, but the fork would not hold the snake without my pushing down on it.

Hissing and spitting, the snake tried to raise up so his fangs could drop and take care of me. That, I was not about to let happen. I leaned my weight hard on the fork, driving it further in between the wooden planks, and kicked off one of my wooden clogs. Reaching carefully for the shoe while the tail of the rattler whipped wildly back and forth, I soon had another weapon in my hand.

The rattling sounds of the rattler were rattling me considerably, but I had grit. I knew what had to be done, so I took that wood shoe with one hand while I bore down on the turning fork with the other, and I beat that old snake till its wicked head popped clean off.

Soon the rattling was still and the snake stopped moving, mostly. Then again I thought of Peachie.

"Peachie? Peachie Fortune!" I called.

Stillness.

I got up and looked around and then recalled the snake coming down the steps to the loft. I looked up fearful into the dark shadows above me and called, "Mistress Fortune?"

No answer.

Over by the door next to the wood box was the ax. I grabbed it in case of more snakes and made my careful way up the steps. There in the loft I found her slumped over my pallet lying on a pile of laundry. The body was stiff when I turned it over and the neck was red and black and swollen from the snake venom, but there was no mistaking who it was. Peachie said we would be the death of her, and she was right.

I whipped around, looking for more snakes and then realized the strangeness of a snake being in the loft in the first place. From the way poor Peachie fell, she must have found the snake coiled in my bedding, but how?

Tabitha! A cat born in May is always bad for bringing in snakes. Weren't Miss Henrietta curing a snake for her henhouse just earlier today? The cat had killed that snake for her mistress, then found another snake in its winter sleep, and brought it still living for me. That cat left a rattler in my bed where I would be sure to find it, only poor Peachie Fortune looking for clean towels had found it instead.

I pulled out a clean sheet from under her and hoisted her stiff body onto my pallet and straightened her out on her back. I could not cover her face, not yet, but I pulled the sheet up to her chin to hide that gruesome neck. With the sheet tucked in and her eyes closed, I could half pretend she was sleeping. I bent down to hear a heartbeat, just in case, then wiped the little wisps of hair from her forehead.

I thought of all the times I watched, bored as dirt, counting as she combed her black hair a hundred times. I remembered the gingerbread and coco on Christmas Day. I remembered our sorting eggshells. At some point I had stopped distrusting and had started depending on her. Why, she was the only friend I had, and now I had no one. That's when I knew I loved her. Like bread loves salt.

Now there was no one to stand between me and the Wicks sisters. Then a deep black pain swept over me. It filled my head, darkening all these pleasing memories, and drove straight down my spine to lodge like wet rock in my gut. I do not know how long I stayed there staring into that old hatchet face of hers. After a while I noticed how outside came little flashes of light. I peered down the steps of the loft to see out the open Dutch door. There it was again. Little flickers of light brightening the evening gloom. I thought of the Wick sisters and how their games of spite and hate had finally gone too far.

I squared my shoulders, for I knew what must done, and that night there would be lightning on Wicked Hill!

CHAPTER XVII: FOXFIRE

*You can become a witch by taking a spinning wheel to the
top of a hill, and waiting until the wheel begins to turn.
The witches will then come to instruct you.*
                                    —2001 *Southern Superstitions*

I took the shortcut through the graveyard of the hired
girls on the way to the cabin. Time to settle up. First with
Miss Marietta!

As I walked, all around me and through the graveyard
rose bubbles of light like tiny stars among the headstones.
Back home we called the little stars foxfire. These danced
about my head and traveled with me through the forest. I
thought of the hired girls buried there. I thought of the one
who died of a fever, and the one who died of a cold, and the
one who died by her own hand. I thought of Dory. And as I
walked the little lights danced round about me.

There was the cabin in the distance under a crescent
moon. Lights like stars hung in midair floating up and
down. The door to the cabin stood ajar. Though this was the
first time ever I recalled it left open, I did not think twice. I
walked right in.

No sooner had I shoved the door wide open than the
ceiling seemed to fall on my head. Something clubbed me!
Was that blood?

I dropped to the floor only to find myself dripping in
wine with the spilt decanter and the silver tray on either
side. The booby trap!

I looked up. There was Miss Marietta glaring at me. "You!"

A glass wine cup smashed above my head.

I scrambled to my feet as another glass shattered on the floor, throwing shards of glass in my face. I covered my eyes with my arms.

A china plate hit my elbow.

"Wait!" I cried. I knew what to do. "Let me show you."

I reached in my apron pocket and pulled out a big eye popper, a fifty-dollar gold piece. I tossed it in the air so she could see it spin. When I caught it, her boney hand shot out and grabbed my wrist. "Oh, no, you don't!" she snapped. I reached in my apron pocket, but her other hand grabbed my fist and pulled it out in the open and pried at it with her gnarled, knobby fingers.

"It's mine!" she snarled. "Give it to me!"

I would not.

"It's mine!" she cried, cupping both her hands around my fist. "Give it to me!" she shouted, but I held on.

"It's mine!" she yelled. We wrestled toe to toe.

"Give it to me," she insisted. "Give it to me!"

And so I did. Once both her hands were cupped around mine, I let go. My hand released its burden that slipped into her startled fingers.

Then Miss Marietta gave out a loud cry. She did not have to look to know what she held. "It's mine," she wailed, opening her palm. In it rested once more the silver penny, sticky as gum and slick as spit. She stared in horror to see her bad luck returned to her.

At first I thought she started to laugh, but the sound was more of a gurgle. She shook all over as if taken with a sudden shock. Her right arm flung out and grabbed her left one. She held onto herself real tight before falling on the floor.

I rushed over and looked down at her keening at my feet. A little pool of spittle spilled down the corner of her mouth.

"She's got the palsy," I said to no one in particular. Just like my maw, I thought, who suffered a great shock when Paw died. First she got the palsy and then died shortly after. Then again, I thought, some live for years. It would be hard. No cook to care for her now, nor servant girl to mistreat, but she had one no-good sister left, which is more than most of us.

Backing up from Miss Marietta there on the floor, I picked my way through the broken plates and shattered glass toward the open door. Lights were twinkling all around the cabin. They turned in circles around me as I marched up the path to the farmhouse. Now for the other!

When I got to the end of the path, thunder rumbled and I realized once more that I was all alone facing that big old house in the dark. Just then a lightning bolt blasted the barnyard no more than ten feet from where I stood. I ran for shelter to the place I feared most, and stood there on the back porch peering into the dim hallway filled with shadows.

I did not want to go in. Run, Amy! I told myself, but if I did, I knew I would take their wickedness with me. I wanted to leave clean. To be rid of them once and for all, I knew there were things that needed to be said and things that needed to be done. Besides, I was not leaving without my wages in any case, so I pulled open the screen door and went inside.

"Miss Henrietta, you there?" I called.

No sound. No sound at all.

"It's me, Miss Henrietta. . . Annamay Scoggins. I've come to take my leave." The long hallway was dark, for I had not been there to light the lamp. I thought I heard a flapping sound in the pantry, but ignored it as a draft on the backstairs. Skitterish, I passed on to the best bedroom where Miss Henrietta slept.

The dying fire in the fireplace gave feeble light. There she was, propped up in bed, eyes wide open, though her body seemed fast asleep. Her chest heaved up and down, and her arms hung at her side, as she snored with her eyes wide open staring into space.

"Miss Henrietta, you funnin' me?" I asked. "You playing possum?"

Miss Henrietta never moved a muscle except for her deep, steady breaths.

I frowned. "Miss Henrietta, your sister is down with the palsy," I said. "Your cook Mistress Fortune is dead from a snake bite. Your cat's gone for good."

Miss Henrietta kept staring out in space, breathing deeply. I walked up to her and stuck my nose in her face. "Miss Henrietta, I got the gold. If you want me to share it with you, you just say so."

Miss Henrietta said not a word, but just kept snoring as her eyes stared straight out into the dark. I walked over to the fireplace. On the mantel was the book of recipes. I picked up the book and looked at my lady once more. "Miss Henrietta, if you don't answer me right now, I'm going to pitch this here book into that there fire." I waited, and then I did.

That strange book with the speckled leather binding took to the fire, and the dying embers shot up in a roaring flame, giving off a strong smell, unlike any animal hide I'd ever smelt before. As I looked down at the fire, I noticed that Old Betsy was not hanging over the hearth.

That's when I dropped to the floor. Miss Henrietta's hands had come up from the shadows, pointing the shot gun that fired at my head.

Lightning crashed outside!

I could see Miss Henrietta still staring out in space, but now rising from her bedside and cocking Old Betsy for another shot. I leapt through the door next to the hearth as a gun blast scattered plaster around my neck and shoulders.

That door led to the little side room next to the hat rack beside the front door. The front door was usually locked and this night was no exception, only the skeleton key was no longer hanging from a ribbon on the hat rack. I rattled the brass door knob in vain. Then I heard a lumbering sound in the dark.

Miss Henrietta, no longer holding the shotgun, walked with her hands straight out in front of her like a sleepwalker, moving her careful way down the long hall. I made for the front room across the hallway, so I could get through to the pantry and out the back like I had done before.

Then a burst of lightning flashed through the front room windows to show me the beaver trap left in the doorway. I stopped short just in time before stepping into its iron jaws.

I heard a sound upstairs; something was flapping in the air just like in the pantry earlier. Could it be that bat? I was thereby distracted when a big arm reached out of the dark to grab me. Miss Henrietta done made it down the hall already and had me by the skirt. I twisted until free and hurried up the staircase to get away from her.

Little did I know of the traps left on the stairs. Mouse traps! Rat traps! Up those stairs I skipped as traps on every step sprung, snapping at my elbows and my neck and hurling themselves over the banister. Miss Henrietta was on her knees, still snoring, but steadily climbing the stairs, blindly reaching out to snatch at my heels.

I did not run too fast, for I wanted her halfway up before I bolted. She was a heavy woman who would take just as long getting down the stairs as climbing up. Either way, once she was halfway upstairs, I could outrun her to the sleeping porch and go through the trapdoor to the pantry and then outside.

The sleeping porch was just a short sprint down the upstairs hall. I rushed through the door to the sleeping porch and was headed toward the trapdoor when I stopped cold in my tracks. There was something in the room with me. I could neither see nor hear any man nor thing. Still I knew someone was there, just as you always know when someone is there. I moved toward the trapdoor, and whatever was in the room countered in the other direction, cutting me off.

I stopped in the darkness to listen.

"Heh," came this wee, whispery voice.

I stood cold in my tracks, listening.

"Heh," the little voice whispered again.

Again I was afraid to answer. As quietly as I could, I moved to the left, and just as quietly something moved to the right.

"Heh . . . heh," came that whispery voice again.

Whatever it was was moving in circles around me, getting closer and closer to where I stood in the dark. On it whispered until it seemed finally to find its voice.

"Amy," it sighed.

I could not help but answer. "What?" I asked fearfully.

"Amy?" it asked, and I wondered if the voice might be friendly, maybe belonging to someone else trapped in this wicked place.

"I'm here," I whispered back.

"Where?" it sighed, and then I got the idea maybe it was not friendly after all, maybe it was only talking to figger out where in the dark I was.

Back and forth we sidled down the long room of the sleeping porch. After a little silence, "Amy," it said. "Amy. . . I'm gonna git you!" it roared.

I felt a rush of air and screamed. No chance of making the trapdoor now, but I was by the door leading to the loom room. I pushed back through the door and shut it. Silence. I leaned my ear against the door. Just then something on the other side rammed the door hard. I jumped back as if slapped. The door knob began to rattle and I remembered the latch.

Finding the door locked, something beat on the door once more, but the door did not give, and then all sounds on the other side died away. Off in the distance I could hear flapping, so I gave it no thought, for I was more afraid of where Miss Henrietta had got to.

I turned to face the gloom of the long room ahead of me. On the far end of that long room stood the door to the hallway. I could make out the opening glimmering in the darkness. Still, I did not hurry, what with traps all around and me in the dark.

There were two ways out as I figgered it. One was to rush down the stairs as soon as Miss Henrietta was all the way upstairs, but the thought of being lost in that dark house once more did not cheer me. The other way was to beat it to the glass door that led to the upstairs front porch. That door was never locked and if need be I could always break the glass to escape. There would be a drop, but I could make it. I settled on the drop.

I took a step forward and heard a creak. Still the room seemed empty, so I took another step, and heard another creak. About that time Miss Henrietta come lumbering past the doorway, arms out as if feeling where I was in the dark. If I just stood still long enough for Miss Henrietta to reach the end of hallway, I could get to the glass door easy. All I had to do was keep still and the dark would hide me.

That's when I heard two creaking sounds. I knew what made the noise. It came from those two cursed spinning wheels. Walking across the floor always made those spinning wheels rock, only this time I had not moved an inch. A thought hit me. What was that about catching a ghost?

That's when the two spinners began to spin on their own, turning their wheels with a rattling whirl like alarms, letting Miss Henrietta know where I was hiding. No time for slyness now. I had to make a run for it and hope the old girl was not close behind.

I slipped out of the loom room and into the upstairs hallway. The glass-paned door leading to the upstairs porch loomed in the darkness. If I could get through the door, I would shinny down one of the three pillars out front and drop to freedom below.

A thunderclap set me to running. Once again, lightning lit up the sky, casting a monstrous shadow on the glass-paned door, for there stood Miss Henrietta Wicks barring the way.

I took a step back and she took a step forward, swaying in the darkness. I feared she might fall on me, and then I would never get up. Instead she blindly reached around and drew forth her reaching stick. She held it in both hands like a well-witcher might hold a diving rod. All around her in the gloom, dust motes swirled in clouds as she lifted her arms while the two spinning wheels clattered behind me. Was I to disappear in a cloud of dust with those two spinners vying to catch my ghost?

No, my lady was not after spirits, she was after flesh. The switch came down hard on my shoulder and tore my smock. I wailed out in pain. Down came the wand again, this time slicing into my face. I put my hand up to my cheek and felt blood.

Oh, have you ever been a poor beaten child on a cold wet day? If so, you will always be that beaten child, however old you get. I fell to my knees and screamed for mercy, knowing full well there was no mercy on Wicked Hill.

Miss Henrietta had me where she wanted me: Upstairs and cornered with no one to stop her and she had the upper hand. I cringed as she raised her arm to whale me once more. Up and down, up and down, she pumped her heavy arm like the arm of a well-sweep. Again and again the blows fell hard on all sides of me as I raised my arms over my head. Miss Henrietta struck blindly, still snoring, with her eyes still open. I whimpered, I whined, I cried, I begged, I pleaded, I promised to foreswear false gods!

A loud rush of air blew down the hallway, like something flapping in the dark. I ducked, and a skittery, twittery shadow headed straight for Miss Henrietta as though to fly right into her. Then all of sudden Miss Henrietta came to her senses. She looked down and saw me and started to laugh.

That big, full-throated chuckle, I knew so well, always poured out when someone was in misery. It made me mad to listen to it. The little beaten child in me hid for a moment, and the fighter in me stood up. I rushed up growling like a feral cat, clawing at her Bedford cord and scratching her face with my nails.

Miss Henrietta never expected that! I don't imagine anyone in fifty years had ever dared touch her. So startled was she that she dropped her reaching stick, and I knew I had her! I grabbed one end of the birch rod and she grabbed the other. We tussled our way downstairs, pulling on that stick, fighting every step. Once I let go, and then the swinging switch cut my hands and stung my head every step of the way down, until on the last step I was able to grab it, and with a mighty pull I wrenched it free.

Mindful of the beaver trap I stepped away toward the center of the hall and weighed the birch rod in my hands. This was the same switch I brung her, that she had used to bewitch her sister. This was the same switch that drew my blood. Here was the heart of her power over me.

There was a thunder clap. "Your secret heart of power is no more!" I cried and broke that reaching stick in two across my knee.

Lightning shot through all the windows, dazzling us with the light. My eyes were so dazzled that I could see Miss Henrietta scrambling to her feet. Clear as day, I could read every look on her face: First shock, then anger, then fear. In fear, she staggered backwards. I heard a snap, and Miss Henrietta commenced to roar. She had stepped into her own beaver trap. With a loud thud she fell to the floor. Yelling and snarling, she tugged at the iron jaws of the trap, as I carefully moved away down the hall.

"Wait!" she cried when she saw what I was doing. "You can't leave me here! You're a good girl. A good Christian girl. You can't leave like that!"

"A good Christian girl," I thought to myself, "don't mean I'm a fool," but what I told her was "Let the dead bury the dead." That's what Davy Snodgrass said the night before I left Fool's Gap.

Well, Miss Henrietta did not like hearing that at all. "And you call yourself a Christian!" she sneered still on the floor. I just kept walking and she started swearing. Miss Henrietta roared in pain, cussing like a Philistine, damning like a prophet.

I paused at the place in the long hall where a candle and matches were always kept. Against my better judgment, I lit the candlestick and set it down on the floor, just out of her reach. No more did I dare do for her.

Then I turned to face her once more. "You'll live," I told her, "for you've got a lot to do. First you got to get your foot out of that trap you set for me. Then you got a sister still living you must care for, and your oldest friend now dead you must bury, and if you want that gold, you must dig up Dory in the cave beneath the sepulcher, and when all that is done, you must repent your wicked, wicked ways and then you must die!"

With that, I showed her my back and, stepping gingerly over the shotgun, made my way outside.

CHAPTER XVIII:
DOWN WICKED HILL

A person that does not believe in witches cannot be bewitched.

—2001 *Southern Superstitions*

The pretty little lights that followed me all about so joyously before were scattered by then, but there was still plenty of light to see. A crescent moon shone overhead. Time to pack my things and skedaddle!

I felt a lump in my throat when I passed by the open cowshed and I felt shivers as I hurried past the dark barn looming in shadows. Hearing the Blue Hollands snoring in the henhouse quieted me somewhat, but truly I did not want to linger. Who knew how long I had on Wicked Hill with both sisters still living?

At the end of the path was the cookhouse now dark inside, but a fire still glowed in the wood stove. I lit the pour lamp and climbed the steps one last time to the loft where I kept my promise to Peachie. I kissed those cold dry lips, and pulled the sheet up over that dear old hatchet face and said good-bye.

I wondered who would dig the grave this time. Let the dead bury the dead, I thought. That's what Davy Snodgrass said the night he begged me to stay, the night before I left Fool's Gap forever. He had begged so hard that he started a coughing fit, and I knew what that meant. First come the cough, then the fever, then the flux. Still, Davy yet lived for all I knew, and that's all what mattered. I don't want to know any different. Ever. I had buried too many already to bury another I loved.

With a sweaty hand, I brushed my hair back. No mirror need tell me what a fright I must have looked with my torn, wine-stained smock and my hair sticking out like a haint. I soothed my curls as best I could. I put on my Polly dress and laced my traveling shoes.

The smock I left on the floor, but since a laborer is worthy of her hire, the apron full of gold I stuffed in my bag. I took the bag in one hand and the pour lamp in the other. Then squaring my shoulders, I made my way down Wicked Hill and into the world at large.

SOURCES FOR
THE BOOK OF RECIPES

2001 Southern Superstitions. Edited by Bill Dwyer. Charlotte,
NC: Aerial Photography Services, Inc. 2004.

Excellent chapbook in the old tradition of chapmen.
This miscellany paraphrases superstitions in a Southern
dialect to give the superstitions their Appalachian
flavor. Grouped in thematic categories the lists suggest
narratives, including this one.

*American Folk Tales and Songs: A Treasury of Lively, Old-Time
English-American Lore.* Ed. Richard Chase. New York:
New American Library-Signet, 1956.

This scholarly miscellany contains many jokes, games,
songs, and tales like that lovely old mountain favorite,
"Like Bread Loves Salt."

Bible: King James Version. London: England, 1611.

This is the King's English referred to often in Appalachia.
The story of Lazarus and Dives can be found in Luke
16:19-31. The verses used in the wine vs. scripture duel
are *"Wine is a mocker, strong drink is raging: and whosoever
is deceived thereby is not wise"* (Proverbs 20: 1), *"And wine
that maketh glad the heart of man, and oil to make his face to
shine, and bread which strengthenth man's heart"* (Psalms
104:15), *"Look not thou upon the wine when it is red, when
it giveth his colour in the cup, when it moveth itself aright,
At the last it biteth like a serpent, and stingeth like an adder"*
(Proverbs 23: 31-32). *"Let the dead bury their dead: but go
thou and preach the word of God" (Luke 9:60).*

Cassell Dictionary of Witchcraft. Ed. David Pickering. London: Cassell, 1996.

This compendium of witch lore focuses on witch trials, primarily British, but also American and European persecutions as well. Many anecdotes are included, especially one about a schoolmaster whose love charm went awry and was followed down his village street by a lovelorn cow.

De Lys, Claudia. *A Treasury of American Superstitions*. New York: Philosophical Library, 1948.

Author provides accurate historical contexts for superstition and provides Freudian analyses to explain witchcraft.

Dorson, Richard M. *Buying the Wind. Regional Folklore in the United States*. Chicago: University of Chicago Press, 1964.

Author supplies riddle of Jack Frost's handkerchiefs left in cabin windows. Also provides anecdotes of witches stealing butter as well as one humorous tale of a farmer overhearing his own animals on Christmas Eve plotting to kill him.

Ferm, Vergilius. *A Brief Dictionary of American Superstitions*. New York: Philosophical Library, Inc. 1965.

A good introduction to the subject, which includes a descriptive account of the Salem Witch Trails of 1692.

Frazer, J. G. *The New Golden Bough*. Cambridge, England, 1900.

The great authority on cultural anthropology provides the distinction between sympathetic and contagious magic. Sympathetic magic is the principle of like to like, whereby an image can produce what it symbolizes, while contagious magic is the ability to   drain the ower of another by taking something that is his.

Hardy, Thomas. "The Oxen." *Poetry of the Victorian Period*. Eds. Jerome Hamilton Buckley & George Benjamin Woods. Glenview, IL: Scott, Foresman and Company, 1965: 932

A footnote to this poem reads: "A widespread folk-belief is that cattle fall on their knees at midnight of Christmas Eve, as did the ox in the stable at Bethlehem when Christ was born."

Hole, Christina. *The Encyclopedia of Superstitions*. New York: Barnes & Noble, 1996.

Mostly British, the superstitions include efficacies of moonwort and mugwort, as well as the authority on life-demanding rivers.

Language of Flowers. Ed. By Gregory C. Aaron. Il. By Pierre-Joseph Redoute. Pennsylvania: Running Press, 1991.

This treasure book thumbnail size contains a brief explanation of British tradition from Elizabethans to Victorians followed with an illustrated list of flowers and their meanings. For instance, a yellow chrysanthemum means decreased affection.

Ovid. *Metamorphoses*. circa 8 A.D.

> The whispery, flapping critter in the farmhouse flew out of a passage from "Orpheus and Eurydice," line 14 reads, *Perque leves populos simulacraque functa sepulcro*, which roughly means "the dead flitted among their funeral busts."

Virgil. *The Pastoral Poems*. 39 B.C.

> In the eighth eclogue can be found an old love charm: *terna tibi haec primum, triplici diversa colore/ licia circumdo, terque haec altaria circum; effigiem duco*, which roughly translated means: "First, I draw these three different colored threads around you three times, and then around the sacrifice three times, and now the effigy three times."